wicked winemakers

CENTRAL COAST
SECOND LABEL
–BOOK FOUR–

SNAPPER'S
Seduction

USA TODAY BESTSELLING AUTHOR
HEATHER SLADE

SNAPPER'S SEDUCTION

© 2025 Heather Slade

This book is a work of fiction. The names, characters, places and incidents are products of the writer's imagination or have been used fictitiously and are not to be construed as real. Any resemblance to persons, living or dead, actual events, locale or organizations is entirely coincidental.

979-8-88649-112-8

Table of Contents

1

Saffron

The October heat in the attic above the Hope Family Winery made sweat trickle down my spine, but I kept sorting through the accumulated boxes and trunks that had been gathering dust for years. I decided to tackle this project just to keep myself busy; otherwise, the stress of the conversation I'd overheard yesterday would eat me alive.

The worst part was that there wasn't anyone I could talk to about it. Dad would deny it. Mom would too, if she even knew, and my older sister, Felicity, and her husband had their own winery in Napa Valley, and she was eight months pregnant. I couldn't burden her with what I'd heard.

The attic stretched the entire length of the main winery building, filled with three generations of accumulation. Wooden crates of ancient bottles and filing cabinets stuffed with correspondence dating back to Prohibition lined the walls, beside trunks of clothing that might have belonged to my great-grandmother or maybe even her mother. I walked over to the single window and tried to open it, but it wouldn't budge.

I wiped away the dust that coated the glass and looked out at our oldest Cabernet block—vines my grandfather had planted decades ago—now gnarled and thick as a man's forearm.

I reached into my pocket for my phone and checked the time. The three hours I'd been up here felt more like six, but there was no point in stopping now, when I had too much time on my hands and too many thoughts swirling through my head. I returned to the same area where I'd started sorting things I unpacked into piles of "keep," "donate," and "trash." So far, the trash pile was winning. Old catalogs from wine equipment suppliers long out of business had been stored in the same boxes as moldy leather ledgers with ink too faded to read. The next box I opened contained a set of brass pipe fittings that might have been for an old bottling line or maybe they were plumbing fixtures. Trash. Definitely.

I was about to open another when a trunk that was shoved far under the eaves caught my eye. The metal corners and leather straps made it look like it belonged on a stagecoach. Inside, wrapped in yellowed tissue paper, were stacks of photographs. Not the color snapshots from the eighties I'd been finding or the Polaroids from the seventies, but black-and-whites mounted on cardboard.

A woman I didn't recognize stood beside old wooden fermentation tanks so unlike the stainless steel we'd been using for as long as I could remember. She wore a dress that screamed nineteen-fifties with its cinched waist and full skirt, had dark hair pinned in victory rolls, and a smile that seemed to leap off the photograph.

Beside her stood another woman, this one with striking features that seemed almost familiar.

I flipped the picture over. In faded blue ink, some-one had written: *Marilyn Hope and Concepción Avila, Christmas Blessing Wine Success, December 1955.*

Marilyn, my father's grandmother, died when my dad was fifteen. I'd never heard of Concepción, but the surname was familiar. Could she be related to the Avilas I knew?

Beneath the photographs lay a leather journal with a brown cover so worn that it was as soft as suede. I opened it with the same care I would use to handle a bird's nest, afraid it might crumble in my hands. Handwriting filled the pages in fountain-pen ink that had faded to sepia. I turned to the beginning and saw it had belonged to Marilyn.

The first entry made me sit back on my heels.

The Christmas Blessing Wine is complete.
What we have created together is something
that could not be accomplished alone. C
brings the wisdom of her Spanish ancestors—
techniques passed down for three hundred
years. I bring what California has taught us,
what this soil whispers to those who listen.

As I kept going, my excitement building with each entry. But as I read more, frustration crept in. The notes were full of cryptic references and half-told secrets.

Temperature must rise with the moon...C knows the timing...blessed on St. Lucy's day with the herbs from her garden...the proportion she guards...seven turns, then twelve, then five...but only when...

Throughout the journal, there were similar references to "C's method" without explaining what it was.

Then I found it—a page that made me pause.

Varietals: Gamay, Syrah, Zinfandel

Method: Carbonic maceration (the French method, as Jules showed us)

Whole clusters only. No crushing. The berries must ferment from within.

I knew the process of carbonic maceration well. We'd experimented with it on small batches of Zinfandel a few years back. The intracellular fermentation that happened inside intact berries resulted in reduced tannins and a bright fruit-forward profile. Best of all, it only took six to eight weeks from harvest to bottle.

Except, so much was missing—varietal percentages, target temperatures, and timing of the various stages.

I was about to keep searching when I noticed two pages stuck together. I separated them as carefully as I could, then read the faded ink.

We have agreed—each of us keeps our portion. What we created can never be made again. Perhaps someday our children and grandchildren will find a way to reunite our efforts.

They'd split the formula. Deliberately. Marilyn kept her part; Concepción kept hers. Neither family could make the wine without the other.

I'd heard of the "Christmas Blessing Wine"—said to have sold out in hours, with those who'd tasted it swearing it was extraordinary. Now, I understood why it had never been recreated—the formula had been split between two families who'd stopped working together. But why?

The historical significance alone was incredible. A wine that rare, if we could reproduce it, would be irresistible to collectors.

The challenges were significant, though. Handpicking only. Mechanical harvesters would crush the clusters. Sealed tanks with CO_2 injection would be needed for the anaerobic environment. But most critical was the formula itself—whatever proportions and techniques Concepción had kept in her half of the recipe.

Rather than put everything back, I gathered the journal and photographs, cleaned up the mess I'd made, then descended the wooden steps that groaned under my feet.

Had it only been twenty-four hours since I stood outside my father's study, eavesdropping on a conversation that stopped me cold?

"I understand the bank's position." His tone had been flat, defeated in a way I'd only heard once before. Three days ago. "But a few bad harvests in a row, then the late frost last spring, taking thirty percent of our tonnage, have put us in a position—"

I'd pressed myself against the wall, barely breathing.

"Ninety days." A long pause. "Yes, I realize that puts us right at New Year's Eve." Another pause. "If we can't bring the account current by then, you'll begin foreclosure." His voice caught. "I see. Yes. Thank you for calling directly, not sending a letter. I appreciate that courtesy."

The next thing I'd heard was the phone hitting the desk as if he'd thrown it.

I was about to walk past when I heard the desk chair creak, then a sound that chilled my blood—my father, Lucas Hope, the man who'd taught me to be strong no matter what, was crying.

I'd backed away silently. *Ninety days.* That was how long we were from losing everything—our home, our heritage, our livelihood.

Like yesterday, I retreated upstairs.

I sat on my bed, with Marilyn's journal, rereading what she'd written about the Christmas Blessing Wine. What seemed like an exciting historical discovery ten minutes ago had just become something more—our only hope, given the time frame.

I grabbed my phone and checked the harvest schedule. Three blocks were left unpicked—designated for a special late-season reserve we'd planned to bottle in spring. Wine that wouldn't matter now if we lost everything in ninety days.

Only Zinfandel, Syrah, and Mourvedre still had grapes on the vine.

My heart sank. We didn't have Gamay, and our Syrah block was tiny, barely a quarter acre.

However, the Avila's Los Caballeros Vineyards had extensive Gamay plantings from Cru's experimental program with Burgundian varietals, and their Syrah was legendary.

I grabbed my laptop and started calculating. To make enough wine to matter—to potentially save us from foreclosure—we'd need at least a thousand bottles. Maybe fifteen hundred if we could manage it.

One ton of grapes yielded roughly seven hundred and twenty bottles. For fifteen hundred bottles, I'd need just over two tons total. If the blend required equal parts of each varietal, that was about three-quarters of a ton of each grape.

We had the Zinfandel. We could harvest three-quarters of a ton easily from our reserve block.

But the Gamay and most of the Syrah? I'd need the Avilas' help for that.

And that was just the grapes. Carbonic maceration required specialized tanks. Ours were all full of this year's conventional fermentation. Los Cab had the capacity. They had empty tanks. The equipment. The space.

I turned back to one of the pages I'd marked and reread what my great-grandmother had written. *We have agreed—each of us keeps our portion.* If the wine was as remarkable as the stories suggested, if we could recreate even a fraction of its magic, we could auction it for premium prices. Beaujolais Nouveau sold for thirty to fifty dollars a bottle at retail. But a one-time recreation of a mythical wine? With the Hope and Avila names behind it?

We could easily ask for two hundred dollars a bottle. Maybe more at the right auction. Fifteen hundred bottles at two hundred dollars each was three hundred thousand dollars. Even if we split it fifty-fifty with the Avilas for their grapes and resources, that was a hundred and fifty thousand for us.

What if we could get four hundred dollars a bottle? Six hundred? Even conservatively, split with the

Avilas, we might clear enough to at least buy time. Maybe push the foreclosure back. Maybe convince the bank we had a plan.

It wasn't perfect. It wasn't guaranteed. But it was something. The only something I had.

My cell phone buzzed. *Three nights to showtime. You know the drill. You with me again this year?*

The text was from Salazar Avila, who everyone called Snapper. Showtime referred to the bachelor auction, a fundraising event held every year at the Wicked Winemakers' Ball—a post-harvest celebration that raised millions for the local Children's Hospital.

"The drill" was an arrangement we'd first made five years ago and every October since. I'd bid, he'd pay, and Isabel Van Orr, who'd been chasing the second-youngest of the six Avila brothers since high school, would be outbid for the fifth time, saving Snapper from having to outmaneuver her relentless pursuit for another three-hundred-and-sixty-five days.

What did I get for my trouble? A favor. One I'd never collected.

This year, I knew exactly what I needed. Multiple things, actually. His family's grapes. Their winery space. Their equipment. Help finding Concepción's half of the formula. And somehow, I had to convince him and his family to partner with me on this without telling my father why. At least not until we had wine ready to sell.

Three nights later, I stood in front of my bedroom mirror, trying to make my hands stop shaking long enough to apply mascara. The black dress I'd worn to the last four auctions hung perfectly, as it always did. Classic lines, expensive fabric from back when we could afford such things, the kind of dress that would never go out of style because it had never really been fashionable. It was appropriate. Respectable. Forgettable. Perfect for someone who didn't want to draw attention.

My phone buzzed with a text from my sister, Felicity. *Wagner surprised me, and we're on our way from Napa. See you soon, pumpkin.*

Pumpkin. She'd given me the nickname when I was twelve and about as round as the orange winter squash. I hated it as much now as I did then.

Felicity had married Wagner Staglin—whose family owned one of the most successful wineries in the valley—five years ago. As a wedding gift from his parents, they were given prime vineyard property and the seed money to start releasing their own vintages. Given the name recognition, their "boutique" operation, which was bigger than ours and our neighbors combined, brought in enough money that my sister could quit her job as a bank teller and become a stay-at-home mom to their son, born exactly nine months after their wedding, and their daughter, who could arrive any minute now. Including at the ball. I smacked my forehead, wondering what Wagner had been thinking with the surprise. He could've flown her down rather than drive.

My phone buzzed again. *Meet you at Sterling in twenty. You ready for this? Don't forget, I owe you one. –S*

For five years, I'd sent back some variation of "ready when you are" or "let's get it done." Tonight, though, would be different, and I couldn't go into it without telling him so.

Forewarning you, I'm collecting this year.

The typing dots appeared immediately. Disappeared. Appeared again.

Wait, seriously? I mean, GOOD! It's about time. So, what's the favor?

Tell you after.

You got it. Whatever you need, Saffron. You know that.

Whatever I needed. But would he feel that way when he learned what I was really asking? When he discovered I needed his family's grapes, their winery, their expertise, and approximately six weeks of intensive collaboration to make a wine that might not even work?

I grabbed my keys and headed for my truck, the journal safe in my purse. The drive to Sterling Creek Winery took ten minutes through hills covered in autumn colors. Every winery I passed was closed early. The ball was the area's biggest charity event of the year, and everyone would be there.

Sterling Creek had been magically transformed with thousands of tiny lights creating a canopy of stars over the entrance, and paper lanterns in burgundy and gold lined the pathways. The barrel room, which could hold five hundred people, was already three-quarters full when I arrived.

"Saffron!" My mother stood near the bar, wearing a navy dress and her mother's pearls, looking every inch the winery matriarch she'd become. Beside her,

Dad wore his best suit—the charcoal one he'd had for a decade but kept in perfect condition.

No one looking at them would guess we were ninety days from disaster.

"You look beautiful, sweetheart," Mom said, kissing my cheek.

"Same dress as always," I said, mentioning it before she could.

"Classic never goes out of style." Dad's hand rested on my shoulder, warm and steady. "The auction should be entertaining tonight. I heard half of this year's bachelors are fresh out of the vineyard."

I laughed. "With four of Alex's brothers married, along with an equal number of their best friends, I'm sure she struggled to get volunteers." Alex—Alexis—was Snapper's older sister. She'd married Maddox Butler, another Central Coast rock star winemaker, a few years ago. They had two kids now, she ran the business side of Demetria, their winery, and still owned half of a wine bar in downtown Cambria, yet year after year, she executed this event flawlessly as if she had nothing to do but devote all her attention to it.

I made small talk with my parents while the room continued to fill. I saw the Avila contingent at their usual table near the front—the five oldest siblings plus their spouses, with their mother Lucia presiding like a benevolent queen. Snapper and his younger brother, Rascon—who everyone called Kick—walked in a few minutes ago but had been waylaid by those seated at every table they passed.

When Snapper looked in my direction, I held up my hand and waved. Even from across the room, the man drew attention. Six-foot-three, shoulders that came from years of ranch work and rodeo, an easy smile that made everyone feel included, and the deepest, darkest, most gorgeous eyes I'd ever stared into. Not that I allowed myself to very often. Snapper and I were friends. That's all we'd ever been or would be, regardless of how he took my breath away and made desire course through my body in a way no other man ever had.

"Felicity!" I heard my mother call out. "You made it."

"When we left the house four hours ago, this sounded like a fabulous idea. Now, I just want a nap." She rubbed her protruding belly and looked around the room.

"Isabel's here," Felicity murmured.

Isabel Van Orr stood near the Avila table, no doubt waiting for Snapper to join his family. The red gown she wore had to have required a team to get her into. Her blonde hair fell in waves that belonged in a shampoo commercial, and diamonds dripped from her ears and throat. She was watching Snapper with the intensity of a cat stalking a bird.

"Same as every year," I said.

"And like before, you'll rescue him." Felicity's eyes sparkled with mischief. "When are you going to make him actually take you on one of the fabulous date he plans?"

"He plans it knowing he'll never have to deliver. Plus, we're friends. He hates dealing with Isabel. I help him out."

"Right. And he just happens to text you to remind you of your deal."

Before I could reply, Alex Avila-Butler took the stage. She commanded attention in a silver gown that caught the lights like moonlight on water.

"Hello, everyone, and welcome to the twentieth annual Wicked Winemakers' Ball. We'll begin dinner service in about thirty minutes to give you all time to check out this year's silent auction. Every year, our generous donors truly outdo themselves, and we're so appreciative of them. Please join me in giving them our thanks."

The room erupted in applause, and Alex left the stage.

"The items offered this year are incredible," my sister's husband said, joining us at the table and flipping through the glossy catalog each guest had been given when we arrived. "That ten-year vertical of Opus One might go for thirty grand."

"At least," my sister agreed as Wagner kissed my mom's cheek, shook my father's hand, then waved in my direction before taking his seat.

"Hey, gorgeous," I heard someone say from behind me at the same moment I felt warm breath against my ear. "You smell amazing," Snapper whispered. "New perfume?"

I glanced over my shoulder and rolled my eyes. "Same shampoo as always, just like the dress I'm wearing."

"As pretty as you are, I guarantee no one's looking at your dress, Saff."

"Be polite and say hello to my sister's family," Felicity scolded. Like Wagner had, Snapper greeted my parents, then waved in Felicity's direction. If my brother-in-law hadn't stood to shake Snapper's hand, it's likely he would've ignored him. Not that Snapper was rude. He was just oblivious at times. A trait that served me well, since it meant he never picked up on the crush I'd had on him most of my life.

"Ma sent me to check out the auction items. Save me a dance after the bidding's over?"

"You know it," I said as he was walking away. He said it every year, and we'd never once danced.

2

Snapper

I was making my way back from the silent auction room when I nearly collided with Felicity Hope, who was waddling toward the ladies' room with one hand pressed to her lower back.

"Whoa, sorry!" I steadied her with a hand on her elbow.

"Snapper." She smiled, though it looked strained. "Isabel just cornered me. She appears determined to win the date with you this year. If she doesn't, I fear she might murder my sister."

I shook my head. "You'd think she would've given up by now."

Felicity laughed, then winced. "God, this baby needs to come out already. I'm so done being pregnant."

"How much longer?"

"Due date is around the end of the month, but the doctor said first babies usually come late." She made a face. "Which means I could be like this for another two weeks—or longer. Mom and Dad are coming up at some point to help us get ready."

"What about Saffron?"

Felicity's expression shifted. "She says she needs to stay and handle the late harvest. You know how she is. Married to that winery." She paused. "But I made her promise that the second I go into real labor, she gets on a plane. Mom and Dad did too. I need my sister there, Snapper."

Her desperation stunned me, and I promised she'd be there, even though I had no idea if that was Saffron's intention.

"Good." She squeezed my arm, then winced again.

Wagner appeared then, looking worried. "You okay, honey?"

"Fine. Just needed to pee. Again." She rolled her eyes. "Third time in an hour."

He wrapped an arm around her and guided her toward the restroom, but she looked back at me. "Whatever's going on with her—help her, okay? She won't ask, but she needs it."

"I will," I told her, wondering if whatever she was alluding to had anything to do with Saffron saying she was calling in a favor this year.

Back at our table, Kick was waiting with that knowing look he always got when he was about to give me shit.

"You know, all you'd have to do is insist she let you take her on the date, given the trouble she goes to every year," he leaned in and said.

I shook my head. "She'd never agree to it."

Kick, who was also my best friend and team-roping partner, shook his head too and muttered under his breath. "You're such an idiot."

While that might be true in most cases, it wasn't when it came to Saffron. If I thought she was the slightest bit interested in being more than friends, I'd jump on the chance to date her. But she wasn't. And rather than risk our friendship by awkwardly asking her out and forcing her to turn me down gently, I refrained.

"Switch seats with me," I said to Kick, pushing away from the table.

"Not a chance. If you don't want to take your shot with the lovely Miss Hope, I sure as hell will. Considering I have the best view of her from where I'm sitting, maybe she and I will make googly eyes at each other throughout dinner."

I stared at him. "Googly eyes? What the fuck is that? Never mind, I don't want to know. Now, unless you have a death wish, quit even *looking* at her and switch seats."

As soon as my other four brothers laughed just as hard as Kick was, I knew he'd set this up before I got to the table. Him adding, "You're such an easy mark," only confirmed my suspicion.

"She'd say yes in a New York minute if you ever got up the nerve to ask," my brother Bit's wife, Eberly, who was seated on the opposite side of me, said quietly enough that only I could hear her. I was about to respond when my sister got up on stage for the second time and asked for everyone's attention.

"Dinner is about to be served, so please take your seats. I hope everyone arrived tonight ready to spend lots of money! Between the fabulous silent auction items I already mentioned and our twenty amazing bachelors ready to charm you into generosity, I'm projecting we'll double the amount we raised last year. Who's with me?"

Several hands went up, along with a rousing round of applause. That was my sister. The woman could talk anyone out of their last dime.

I looked over at Saffron's table, hoping to catch her eye. What I saw instead made me wince. The girl I'd rarely seen without a smile was lost in thought, looking like someone had kicked her metaphoric puppy. What in the hell was that all about? On the plus side, since she hadn't noticed yet, I could keep staring as long as I wanted.

When I told her she was so pretty no one would be looking at her dress, I'd meant it. Three years ago, when I'd complimented her on it, it was the first time she told me it was the same gown she always wore. The next year, when I offered to buy her another in exchange for bidding on me, I wasn't sure what had been worse—how mad she was at me, or the hurt look on her face her anger was meant to hide.

Tonight, she wore her hair down, which I preferred over the ponytail I usually saw her in. The mahogany strands fell on her bare shoulders, making me long to sweep them away and kiss the skin they were lucky enough to touch. I was about to look away when her eyes met mine and I was held mesmerized by the pain so clearly etched on her face. It made me want to get up, ask her to join me outside, make her tell me what was wrong, then fix it. All of it. Every single thing that hurt her. If she'd let me, I'd make it my life's mission.

"Isabel van Orr? Where are you, sweetie?" I heard my sister say after the dinner plates were cleared.

"Here I am," Isabel said over the noise of the crowd, not that I'd look in her direction. I knew damn well where she was sitting, just like Alex did. What I didn't know was what kind of shit my sister was about to stir up.

I scowled in her direction as a warning, not that she'd heed it, ever. She winked at me, then looked back at Isabel.

"Promise me that this will be the year you outbid everyone for a date with my little brother, Izzy."

"You know I will, Al."

Everyone at our table, myself included, chuckled at the two women's use of nicknames they hated equally. Just like Saffron hated it when her sister called her pumpkin.

My gaze was drawn to her again, but when I looked that way, Saffron was gone. Where in the hell was she?

"Excuse me," I muttered, tossing my napkin on my chair after I stood. Rather than cut through the crowded tables, I left the main room through one of the archways and made my way out to the bar, hoping that was where I'd find her.

"Hey, Snapper. What can I get you?" the guy behind it asked.

"Bourbon neat," I said as I surveyed the otherwise empty room.

"Looking for someone?" the guy asked.

I shook my head, then changed my mind. "Saffron Hope. You know her?"

"Yeah, I saw her a minute ago. I think she was on her way to the silent-auction tables."

"Thanks," I said, walking away and leaving my drink on the bar.

Sure enough, she was coming out of the room as I was going in.

"Bid on anything?" I asked.

"No. It's all too rich for my blood this year." She smiled, but it didn't meet her eyes.

I took her hand and led her back in. "Come on. Show me what caught your eye. I owe you, remember?"

"And I told you I plan to collect this year." The second fake smile she sent me made me grind my teeth.

I took a step closer, squeezing her hand rather than dropping it. "Whatever you want, Saffron."

She removed her fingers from my grasp. "I should get back to the table."

"Wait!" I called out when she spun around and stalked away. When she didn't stop, I hurried and got in front of her. "Aren't you going to tell me what it is?"

Her brow furrowed. "I said I'd tell you after."

"Whatever it is must be a doozy, then," I joked. Not that her expression indicated she found it funny.

When she walked away again, I let her go, then circled around to the bar. My bourbon sat waiting, and when I didn't see the bartender, I tossed it back and dropped a twenty, determined to get to the bottom of what was up with Saffron before the night came to an end.

Rather than take a seat, I stood in the archway, listening as Alex announced the name of the first bachelor. That I'd never even heard of the guy had to mean I was too old for this shit. Next year, I'd turn my sister down flat. Five years was fucking enough, especially since the money she raised from my bid came out of my own pocket. Not that I minded. I'd still donate that much or more if she'd let me off the hook of this farce.

The early bachelors went quickly. A tech entrepreneur sold for four thousand to a wine industry venture capitalist's daughter, and a sommelier Alex had convinced to come up from Santa Barbara fetched five grand from a local restaurant owner. The next guy up, whose family had purchased one of the larger vineyard estates last year, caused a minor bidding war between three women that ended at twelve thousand with a lot of good-natured laughter. The rest, I tuned out.

"And now, ladies, a crowd favorite returning for his fifth year. My brother tried to hide in the back, but we see you, Snapper! Come on up here!" Alex's eyes sparkled with mischief.

I made my way to the stage, shaking my head at her theatrics. Rather than take a direct route, I weaved my way through the tables, past where the Hopes sat.

"Got your paddle ready?" I whispered in Saffron's ear.

"She told me she's starting the bidding at twenty thousand," Felicity teased.

"I'm worth at least double that, right?" I nudged Saffron, and she rolled her eyes. I counted that as a win. Anything was better than another half-assed grin.

"Salazar 'Snapper' Avila," my sister began as I got closer to the stage. "Is a championship team roper, an accomplished winemaker, and yes, ladies, he's single. Though I should mention he's currently recovering from a shoulder injury, so maybe keep the date activities low-impact." She paused to give the audience time to laugh.

"Thanks for making me sound fragile, Alex," I said into the microphone, wishing she'd just get on with it so I could head back over to Saffron's table.

"Bidding starts at five thousand dollars," Alex announced.

"Ten thousand." Isabel's response cut through the room.

"Twelve thousand," called another woman, who I couldn't see through the bright stage lights but knew wasn't Saffron.

"Fifteen." Isabel countered.

The bids went back and forth, each one upping a grand, but by twenty thousand, most had given up, and Saffron hadn't bid once.

"We have a bid of twenty. Anyone want to raise it to twenty-five?" Alex called out.

"I will," said Isabel, even though hers was the last bid.

"Twenty-five thousand going once," Alex started.

Just when I started to get nervous, Saffron raised her paddle. "Thirty."

Isabel's head turned in that direction as if to challenge her. "Thirty-five thousand."

"Forty."

"Fifty." A minute ago, Isabel had sounded bored. Now, she was annoyed.

Saffron raised her paddle. "Sixty."

Isabel pushed away from the table and stood. "Seventy thousand."

I looked out at Saffron, who, for the first time, was looking at me. I raised a brow.

"Seventy-five thousand."

Gasps echoed through the barrel room. Even Alex looked shocked.

Isabel's face flushed red, and she looked from Saffron to me, then back again.

"Seventy-five thousand going once," Alex said slowly. "Going twice..."

Isabel's voice could have frozen wine in the barrel. "You can have him."

"Sold to bidder number forty-seven for seventy-five thousand dollars!" Alex shouted, not bothering with the rest of the countdown.

The applause was deafening, but I was in no mood to play up the crowd, not when I saw Saffron get up and leave her table. I jumped off the stage and rushed in her direction. Not fast enough, though. Isabel beat me to her.

"Seventy-five thousand? Are you fucking kidding me, Saffron?" I heard her say as I approached. "We all know you can't afford that kind of money." Saffron didn't bite back. "I guess you're hoping that, this time, he'll marry you. Fat chance of that. Whatever will you do when he doesn't? More, what will your daddy do?"

I'd heard more than enough and took a step forward. "Everything okay here?" I stepped closer to Saffron than Isabel and rested my hand on the small of her back.

Isabel straightened, and her smile switched to high beam. "Of course! I was congratulating Saffron on her win. Seventy-five thousand dollars—you must have quite the evening planned."

Likely knowing I'd heard what she said, Isabel walked away.

"Come with me," I said, taking Saffron's hand like I had earlier.

"I'm leaving. We can talk tomorrow."

I didn't stop walking until we were outside. "You leave without telling me what's going on. I follow."

She removed her hand from mine, and I let her, knowing if she dashed off toward her truck, I'd beat her there.

"I have a headache. I don't want to be here. I'll talk to you tomorrow."

"No," I said, softening my tone when I saw the tears she was trying damn hard to hide. "Tell me what you need, and it's yours.

"Tomorrow," she said again. "Meet me at the Olallieberry Diner at ten."

I wanted to argue. More, I wanted to take her in my arms, find out why she was on the verge of crying, then make whatever was upsetting her go away. Instead, I gave in. "Tomorrow. Ten AM. And if you're not there, know that I'll have the sheriff put out an APB on you."

That got a half smile. "Vader wouldn't do that."

"You don't know the favors he owes me."

The smile was gone. "Don't worry, Snapper. I'll be there."

I let her walk away, and as she did, I swore I heard her add, "I have no choice."

3

Saffron

When I arrived at the Olallieberry Diner at nine forty-five, the morning fog had rolled in from the Pacific, wrapping Moonstone Beach Drive in a gray blanket that muted the crash of waves across the road. Through the diner's windows, warm light spilled onto the sidewalk, and I could see the breakfast crowd filling most of the red vinyl booths.

My stomach churned. Not from hunger—I couldn't eat if I tried—but from what I had to do in the next hour. Ask Snapper Avila, the man who made my heart race every time he walked into a room, to save my family. Without letting him know we needed saving.

The smell of bacon grease and coffee, along with the comforting chaos of clinking plates and morning conversations, wrapped around me when I walked inside. Marcy Delgado looked up from behind the counter and grinned. We'd gone to high school together, though she'd been two years ahead of me. Her dark hair was up in a messy bun, and she had new purple streaks that hadn't been there the last time I was here.

"Saffron! I haven't seen you in here for weeks." She grabbed a menu. "Table for one, or are you meeting someone?"

"There will be two of us, thanks."

She wriggled her eyebrows. "Snapper Avila, by any chance?"

My cheeks heated. "It's not like that, Marcy."

"Sure, it's not." She tilted her head toward the back. "Want your usual seat?"

"Please."

She led me to the corner booth where I'd sat through too many heartbreak coffees with my sister to count. The vinyl, while replaced not that long ago, was already showing signs of wear. Above me, faded photographs of Moonstone Beach decorated wood-paneled walls, and someone had strung the tiny shells between the frames after they'd fallen down last Christmas.

I took Marilyn's journal out of my bag and set it on the table, then changed my mind and put it back. I didn't want to appear too eager.

"Coffee while you wait?" Marcy had returned, pot in hand.

"Please. With cream."

She poured and set a small bowl of creamers on the table. "How's the family?"

"Same ol', same ol'," I said. "How about yours?"

"Dad's as stubborn as ever." She shook her head. "Mom wants him to slow down, and he tells her he isn't dead yet."

She chuckled, then headed off to refill other cups. I dumped three creamers and an equal number of sugar packets into my mug and stirred, watching the cream swirl.

The bell above the door chimed, and Snapper filled the doorway, scanning the diner until he saw me. Behind him, the fog had started to lift, and weak sunlight outlined his frame. My breath caught. Last night in his tux, he'd been devastating in a polished, untouchable way. This morning? The faded jeans that hung low on his hips and the charcoal-gray Henley that clung to his chest and arms had my focus unraveling. The fabric stretched across his shoulders when he raised a hand to push his hair, still damp from a shower, back, and when he smiled at me, my traitorous heart flipped. Did the man have to be the very definition of hot-as-fuck?

Stop it, I scolded myself. He's here as a friend. Nothing more.

He made his way through the tables with an easy grace that came from years of this place being his second home, just like it was mine. I noticed how women's heads turned to track his movement as he dodged a toddler who'd escaped his high chair and stepped aside for a waitress balancing a full tray. Of course they stared, not that he noticed. Snapper had absolutely no idea the effect he had on people. Especially on me.

"Good morning, sweetheart," he said, sliding into the booth, across from me. The endearment meant nothing. He called everyone sweetheart, darlin', or honey.

"Morning."

Marcy appeared at our table. "Hey, Snapper. How's that shoulder?"

"Getting better, thanks." He smiled up at her. "How's the breakfast rush treating you?"

"Same chaos as always." She tapped her notepad with her pen. "Coffee?"

"Black, please. And I'm starving—can I get the lumberjack special with extra bacon, eggs over easy, wheat toast, and a side of buttermilk pancakes? Oh, and two olallieberry muffins, heated."

"I don't know where you put it all, Avila. Some day, it'll catch up with you," she commented.

He rubbed his stomach. "Still got my washboard abs, don't I?"

She laughed. "Yeah, you do." She turned to me. "What about you, Saff?"

"Just coffee, thanks."

Snapper's eyes scrunched. "When's the last time you ate?"

"Last night—"

"No, you didn't." His gaze sharpened. "You didn't touch your dinner."

"I'm not hungry."

"She'll have scrambled eggs and wheat toast."

"Dammit, Snapper, I said I wasn't hungry."

Marcy looked between us, then scribbled on her pad. "How about I bring an extra plate?" She walked away, shaking her head, not waiting for either of us to argue.

Snapper rested his forearms on the table. "What's got you tied up in knots?"

"Nothing. I just don't feel like eating."

His nostrils flared, but he sat up and rested against the booth. "So, what's the favor?"

I set the journal on the table. "Does the name Concepción Avila mean anything to you?"

His expression shifted to curiosity. "She's my great-grandmother on my father's side. Why?"

"I found this in our attic a few days ago." I opened the journal to the page I'd marked. "It was my great-grandmother Marilyn's, and in it, she mentions something about her, Concepción, and their husbands making wine."

"The Christmas Blessing?"

"Yes. Exactly," I said, somewhat surprised he knew about it.

"It's been a long time since anyone's mentioned it. Everyone thought it was an urban myth."

"According to this, I think it was."

He leaned forward, and I turned the journal around. His finger traced what was written and I watched those hands, trying not to imagine them touching me with the same focus.

"Wow. This is wild," he muttered. "So, how does this relate to all the favors I owe you?"

I flipped through the pages. "Here, my great-grandmother says that she kept her half and Concepción kept hers. She goes on to say something about maybe having a falling out and that's why the wine was only made once."

Snapper's food arrived in a clatter of plates. The lumberjack special covered half the table—eggs, bacon, sausage, hash browns, and a stack of pancakes that could feed three people.

"This is incredible," Snapper said, but I wasn't sure if he meant the food or the journal. He picked up his fork, then set it down and pushed his plate of bacon between us. "Have some of this."

I picked up a strip to appease him. The salt and grease actually tasted good enough that I reached for another piece.

"I keep asking what the favor is, and you keep avoiding answering me." He cut into his pancakes, but his eyes stayed on me.

"I need you to find Concepción's half of the formula."

"Of course." No hesitation. No questions about why or what for. Just instant agreement. "When were you thinking of making it? Next year's harvest?"

"No." I grabbed another strip of bacon from his plate, needing something to do with my hands. "It has to be this Christmas."

He set down his fork. "Next year maybe, but this year would be impossible."

"You're wrong. The journal says they used carbonic maceration—"

His finger moved down the list, stopping at each grape varietal. "Gamay, Syrah, and Zinfandel—those would work. But still…" He shook his head, and when a lock of dark hair fell across his forehead, my fingers itched to brush it back. "This takes planning—"

"We have Zinfandel. A reserve block we left unpicked for late bottling. And we have some Syrah, but not much—maybe a quarter acre."

"But no Gamay."

"Right. And not enough Syrah." I met his gaze directly. "I need your Los Caballeros' grapes."

He rested against the back of the booth. "That's not a small ask."

"I know. And there's more." I might as well lay it all out. "I need winery space—our tanks are all full from this year's fermentation. I need the carbonic maceration equipment, the CO2 injection systems, and I need a crew for handpicking. The clusters have to stay completely intact, which means no mechanical harvesting."

"Jesus, Saffron." He ran a hand through his hair. "This isn't just a favor. This is—"

"A partnership," I finished. "Fifty-fifty split on everything. The costs, the work, the profits. Both families, just like the journal says."

"The part about both families is interesting," he said, returning to the journal. "Sounds like our grandmothers each had specific knowledge that had to be combined."

"That's why I need you to find Concepción's half. The percentages, the temperatures, the timing—whatever else she kept in her notes." I reached over and tore a piece off of one of his pancakes. The olallieberry syrup he'd poured over them was tart-sweet and perfect, but I barely tasted it. "Can you please just look for anything Concepción might have left behind? Papers, journals, formulas?"

His dark eyes searched mine as he watched me eat his food. "I don't understand the rush, sweetheart. What aren't you telling me?"

Everything. I'm telling you absolutely nothing that matters.

"I just…I want to do this, and I don't want to wait."

His fingers drummed against the table. But before he could push harder, the waitress reappeared with more coffee.

"How's everything?" she asked.

"Great," Snapper said, not looking away from me. "Can we get another short stack of the olallieberry pancakes?"

"She always eats half your food. I'd think you'd know that by now."

I looked between the two of them. "I didn't—"

"You did, and the second order is for me, not you." While what he'd said was harsh, the way he spoke— soft and knowing—made my heart skip a beat. If I didn't know better, I'd add loving. But I *did* know better. Snapper was kind to everyone. I wasn't special.

Marcy walked away shaking her head. I looked down at his food. I'd eaten more than I realized. The bacon was gone, most of his pancakes, and I'd made a serious dent in his hash browns. "Sorry," I muttered.

"I don't care about the food, Saffron. You keep eating, and I'll keep ordering more."

I held up both my sticky hands. "I promise I won't."

"You will, but like I said, I don't give a shit."

"You sound like you do."

"No. I don't. What I want is for you to talk to me." He lowered his voice. "Whatever's going on, I can help."

His hand moved across the table, stopping just short of reaching for mine. The gesture was so Snapper—offering comfort while respecting boundaries. That space between our hands felt like the Grand Canyon and a whisper all at once.

"There's nothing to tell."

His hand withdrew, and I could see the flex of his forearms where he'd pushed up his sleeves and the way his chest rose and fell with each breath. Even the way he held his coffee mug—fingers wrapped around it completely—made heat pool low in my belly.

Marcy set the second stack of pancakes in front of him a few minutes later, then walked away without saying anything else.

Snapper pushed them across the table.

"You said those weren't for me."

"I lied. Now, tell me what's going on."

I clutched the journal to my chest. My desperation had to be showing. The naked need for this to work.

"All right. I'll do it," he said. "But, Saffron?" His eyes bored into mine. "Whatever you're holding back, whatever has you so worked up—you can tell me. You know that, right?"

A long silence stretched between us. The diner noise faded to background static, and I couldn't speak.

He reached for my hand, his gaze never leaving mine. "I'll grant your favor, but *this* is how it's gonna go down."

4

Snapper

I almost took the words back; that was how hard the look on her face hit me. Whatever the fuck was going on with her was bad. Except nothing I imagined made any sense.

"I'll grant your favor," I said again. "But we're gonna do it my way."

She clutched her great-grandmother's journal tighter against her chest. "What do you mean?"

"This isn't a decision I can make alone. You're asking for a ton and a quarter of Los Caballeros grapes, our winery space, our equipment, and a crew. That involves my brothers—especially Cru, since he manages the vineyards. I need to talk to them first. Get their buy-in."

"Of course," she murmured, but her face had paled.

God, I wished she'd just talk to me about what made her react that way. For now, though, I'd let it go. Later, once I knew if what she was asking could even be done, I'd press the issue.

"I'll see if he and Daphne are available now, then get back to you."

"Understood."

When her eyes filled with tears, I reached across the table and took her hand. "I'll do everything I can to make this happen. I promise."

She tried to pull her hand away. I squeezed her fingers. "Know this, Saffron; this matters to you, which means it matters to me too."

"Thank you," she said so quietly I had to strain to hear her.

When she squeezed my fingers back, an inexplicable sense of relief overcame me, and with it, another feeling I'd been pushing down for far too long. It was time I let it rise to the surface and did something about it. While I admitted that she mattered to me—in a roundabout way at least—the truth was, the way I felt about her went far deeper. I wanted Saffron in my life and not just as a friend or a hookup. I wanted more. A *helluva* lot more, and if we were going to spend the next six to eight weeks working side by side, maybe she'd see me as more too. More than the guy she bid on every year to save him from Isabel's clutches. Maybe as a man she could be interested in.

"What are you thinking about?" she asked.

You. How I'm ready to go all in—not that I could say any of that.

"Everything I need to do today. Who I need to talk to."

While she indicated she agreed, I saw the skepticism in her expression. She always called me out on my shit. Except now, she wouldn't. And dammit if I wasn't more than happy to take advantage of it.

The thought should've felt wrong. She was asking for help, not hitting on me. But I'd been half in love with this woman since we were teenagers, and I was tired of keeping my distance because I thought she wasn't interested. If she needed me, I'd be there. And if spending every day together gave me a shot at showing her how I felt? I'd take it.

I stood and took my wallet out, leaving enough cash on the table to cover our meal three times over. "I'll call you later."

"Okay." She sounded uncertain.

"Hey." I waited until she looked up at me. "We'll make this work. If it isn't with our grapes, with someone else's."

The ghost of a smile touched her lips. "I hope you're right."

We walked out to the parking lot where my truck sat next to her beat-up Ford.

Every instinct screamed at me to pull her into my arms, to promise her everything would be okay, to kiss away the worry lines etched between her brows. But I couldn't. Not yet.

"Drive safe," I said instead.

She climbed into her vehicle and I stood there, watching until her taillights disappeared around the curve, then got into my own SUV and headed for Los Cab.

When I arrived at the main house, my mother's car was in the driveway, along with Cru's truck. Since he and Daphne lived a few minutes' walk from the main house, my guess was Ma had a honey-do list for him, and that's why he'd driven over.

I was headed toward the porch steps when I heard another vehicle approaching. I looked over and saw Bit pull in. While Sunday was family dinner day, people didn't usually start showing up until late afternoon.

"How's it going?" I asked when he climbed out.

"Cru needs some help with the water heater. I don't know why Ma didn't call me in the first place, since I'm the one who fixed it the last time. What about you? Why are you here?"

"I need to talk to Cru and Daphne about something."

"What?" he pressed.

I kicked at the dirt in the driveway. Bit had the kindest, gentlest soul of anyone I knew, so his direct approach had never bothered me. In fact, running into him first was probably a good thing. I could explain it all to him before Cru and get his take on it.

"Saffron Hope just asked me for a massive favor."

"What kind of favor?"

I laid it all out—the Christmas Blessing Wine, the grapes, the equipment, the partnership, the insane timeline. "It's weird, Bit. She's desperate. Scared even, and I can't figure out why."

"I've heard some things," he said as we walked toward the house.

"What?"

"About Hope Family Winery." He rested against the rail of the porch steps. "They're in trouble."

"How bad?"

"Foreclosure."

"Jesus Christ," I said under my breath.

"I don't know all the details, but from what I've heard, the bank is ready to act."

Everything clicked into place. The desperation. The tears. The insistence that it had to be this Christmas. Which meant I had to convince my brothers and sister to go along with it.

"What would you do?"

He put his hand on my shoulder. "For the woman I loved? Everything humanly possible."

"Is it that obvious?"

Bit chuckled. "To everyone but you. At least until now."

My eyes widened. "Everyone?"

"Except you *and* Saffron."

We found Cru exactly where Bit said he'd be: in the basement, looking at the water heater.

"Time to replace it," Bit muttered.

"Figured that out," Cru responded. "I got one on the way. I'm just trying to piece this one together enough that Ma can get through until tomorrow."

"Let me do it. Snapper needs to talk to you."

Cru looked up at me, then moved out of Bit's way.

"What's up?" he asked after I led him up the cellar steps and out onto the porch.

I reiterated everything I'd just told Bit.

When I finished, Cru leaned against one of the barrels and crossed his arms. "That's quite an ask."

"I know. Do we even have the grapes?"

He thought for a moment. "Yeah. We've got Gamay in Block 9—about two acres that we planned to let hang longer for a late-harvest project. And the Syrah in Block 12 is still on the vine. We could spare three-quarters of a ton of Gamay and the same amount of Syrah without impacting our production targets."

"What's the timeline on ripeness?"

"The Syrah needs another week, maybe ten days. The Gamay, closer to two weeks. If she's got Zinfandel that's ready sooner, we could do this in three waves."

"Equipment?"

"We have a couple of tanks that aren't being used that would work for carbonic maceration. The CO2 injection systems are all functional." He paused. "Space won't be an issue either. The east wing of the cellar has room."

"So we can do it."

"Technically, yes."

Technically. The word said plenty. "But we need to get the go-ahead from the rest of the siblings."

"It's only fair. That Saffron's willing to split the profits should be enough. Still, I wouldn't feel comfortable unless we took it to them," he agreed.

I pushed off the porch rail. "There's another issue we need to talk about."

"What's that?"

"According to Bit—"

"They're about to go under," Cru finished for me.

"I guess you heard too."

"I did and my guess is that Saffron wants to do this without Lucas knowing."

"She hasn't admitted the financial trouble to me, but yeah, that would be my guess too."

"If that's the case, then we need to think about the crew we use."

He was right, and that wasn't something I'd considered. We could hardly ensure the day workers we brought in for the harvest would keep what we were doing confidential. They moved from vineyard to vineyard during the harvest, and it would be too much to ask.

"Got any ideas?"

Cru looked up at me and grinned. "Of course I do."

"You gonna tell me?"

"Los Caballeros," he said quietly. "If we're going to pull this off without Lucas finding out, at least until Saffron is ready to tell him, we'll need absolute discretion, and that means calling in both current members and the *Viejos*."

"Understood. What's the next step after we talk to our sibs?"

"Don't wait. They'll agree. It's just courtesy that you're asking. Call an emergency meeting now. Preferably for this afternoon, since everyone's still in town from last night's ball." Cru put his hand on my shoulder. "This is what we do, Salazar. We help those in need even when they don't know they need it. Especially one of our own."

He took out his phone, sent a group alert, then waited as responses came in. "Everyone who's in town will be at the caves in ninety minutes. Which means you need to get our brothers and sister here before that."

"On it. You said everyone who's in town. Who isn't?"

"Van Orr is in Europe, and Cullen is in Australia."

"Right. What about Lucas?"

"I took him off the distro list for now." He'd looked away, but turned to face me. "Glad to see you wised up."

My eyes scrunched. "What're you talking about?"

"You and Saffron. 'Bout time." He slugged my shoulder, and I laughed. "Yeah, Bit said the same thing."

"Is she on board?"

"If you mean is she into me as much as I'm into her, then no. Not yet anyway."

"She is. She's just as unwilling to admit it as you were."

"So seriously, it's that obvious?"

"Since high school, bro."

My brothers all arrived within a few minutes. Alex said she couldn't get here right away but to video her in for whatever I wanted to talk about. I did, and as Cru predicted, everyone was all in.

Los Caballeros had been part of my life since birth. The secret society dated back centuries—to our grandfathers' grandfathers and beyond. The name itself connected us to the Knights Templar, the medieval warriors who'd defeated the Moors and taken control of Jerez in southwestern Spain. They'd renamed it Jerez de los Caballeros. Jerez of the Knights.

When our ancestors immigrated to America in the late 1860s, they brought the society with them. They'd settled first in Napa Valley, then moved down to the Central Coast, where they'd replaced the apple orchards with grapevines. Soon after, my family started Los Caballeros Vineyards and Winery. Since the property had natural caves, those were developed for barrel storage, and at the same time, a secret meeting room was added. According to a sign carved of wood that hung in the space, the first gathering was held in 1865.

Eleven members currently served. My oldest brother, Brix, led us now that Tryst had stepped down.

He'd earned his nickname as a teenager when he became obsessed with measuring degrees Brix, the sugar content in grapes that determined optimal harvest timing. Our father thought it fit him perfectly.

The rest of us—Cristobal, Cru, Bit, Kick, me, along with Noah and Dalton Ridge, Press and Beau Barrett, and Zin Oliver—formed the active brotherhood. We met only when necessary, usually when someone needed our help, like now. We used our wealth, our connections, and our resources to protect our own. Sometimes we operated outside the law, but regardless, always in secret.

The *Viejos* were the generation before us. Tryst had served as their leader after our father, Alfonso, died. The others—Hewitt Ridge, Martin Barrett, Michael Oliver, Charlie Jenson, Lucas Hope, Malcolm Warwick, Noah Cullen, and Baron Van Orr—were the remaining elders.

The temperature dropped twenty degrees as soon as I stepped inside the caves' entrance. I'd spent a lot of time in here over the years—for wine events, parties, and of course, Los Caballeros meetings. But this would be the first time I was the one requesting help. I watched everyone enter and take their places around the large round table that dominated the center of the room—solid oak, scarred by centuries of use, surrounded by high-backed chairs that had been here longer than I'd been alive. Sconces on the walls provided light, and a single ventilation shaft in the ceiling ensured we wouldn't suffocate.

After all those expected had arrived, we remained standing. Brotherhood protocol dictated we wait for the leader to call the meeting to order.

Brix made eye contact with each of us in turn. Then with each of the *Viejos*. Tryst last.

"Los Caballeros," he began. "We're here this morning because our brother needs our help."

The *Viejos* took their seats, and out of respect, the current members stood behind them.

Brix turned to me. "Go ahead."

My mouth went dry. Public speaking had never been my strong suit—that was more Brix's territory. But this was too important to fumble.

"Earlier today, Saffron Hope came to me with a request." I reached for my phone and brought up the photo I'd taken of the journal page. "She found this in her great-grandmother's attic—evidence that in 1955, Marilyn Hope and Concepción Avila, along with their husbands, created a wine called the Christmas Blessing."

I handed my phone to Brix, who viewed the image before passing it along.

"The wine was remarkable. Made only once. Sold out in hours. Those who tasted it said it was extraordinary." I paused. "Saffron wants to recreate it. This year. To have it ready by Christmas."

"That's six to eight weeks," Cristobal said. "Barely doable even with carbonic maceration."

"I know. But the point is, it is possible. Cru's confirmed we have the grapes she needs, along with the equipment and space."

"What do you need from us?" Zin asked.

"This endeavor must be undertaken with the utmost secrecy."

The room remained quiet; I hadn't expected anyone to disagree.

"And that means, we need a crew. We'll be harvesting three varietals in separate pickings over the next fourteen days."

"Handpicked?" Tryst asked.

"That's right."

He motioned to Brix, who stood behind him. When he moved to the side, Tryst pushed his chair from the table and got to his feet. "In the last five years, wine sales worldwide have drastically decreased from the highs we previously experienced. Many of us here today have struggled in the same way we all know the Hope family is now."

Was I the only one here who hadn't been aware of their predicament?

"We also know that Lucas Hope will not come to us for help."

Malcolm Warrick, who'd come close to losing his own home and winery less than a year ago, spoke up. "No one understands his position better than I do. I would not have come to you either if it hadn't been for my daughter and son-in-law." Malcolm's eyes met Bit's. The acceptance and appreciation on his face was met with Bit's obvious affection for the man.

"There's one other thing I should mention. Saffron isn't aware that I know about the foreclosure. Like her father, she's a proud woman, whom I'm giving the time and space to tell me when she's ready."

"Spoken like a man in love," my brother Kick said under his breath.

Tryst raised a brow. "Spoken like an *honorable* man."

I was humbled by my uncle's praise. I was nine years old when my father passed away from a sudden heart attack, and Tryst had stepped in as his surrogate. "Thank you," I said to him.

"There's one other thing I need to point out. The journal Saffron found contained only the varietals used in the wine. What we don't have is the formula that would include the percentages used."

More murmurs went around the room. I waited until it quieted down, then continued.

"Saffron found another passage that I'll read aloud. 'We have agreed—each of us keeps our portion. What we created can never be made again. Perhaps some-day our children and grandchildren will find a way to reunite our efforts.'"

Unlike many other things I'd said thus far, what I read next was met with surprise. "As you can imagine, there hasn't been much time for us to search for the missing formula. Saffron and I will be undertaking that while also planning the harvest."

"We can help," Bit offered.

More murmurs of agreement went around the room.

"Whatever we can do to ensure this wine gets made will be greatly appreciated."

Tryst stood slowly. "Excuse me for a moment." He left and retreated farther into the caves. When he returned, he was carrying something wrapped in cloth.

He set it on the table in the center of our circle and unwrapped the fabric.

A wine bottle. Old, dusty, the label faded, but still legible—*Christmas Blessing Wine, 1955.*

"Holy shit," Kick muttered.

"This is the only known bottle in existence," Tryst said. "It's been in the rare room for as long as I can remember. Worth a small fortune to collectors, but worth more for what it represents."

I stared at the bottle, my mind racing.

"You could have the contents analyzed," Tryst continued. "Modern technology can identify every varietal, every percentage, perhaps even fermentation temperatures. But understand—once you open it, it's gone forever. The only bottle of Christmas Blessing Wine that I know of will cease to exist."

The weight of that settled over me.

"May I?" Bit asked, reaching for the bottle.

"Of course," said Tryst.

My brother held it up to the light, studying the wine through the dark glass. "If we don't open it and Hope Winery goes under, this bottle becomes nothing but a reminder of what could have been both then and now. The wine was supposed to be a blessing. The name itself says so. How does something kept in a bottle for over seventy years bless—benefit—anyone?" He set it down carefully. "But if we open it, if we use it to save the legacy…doesn't that honor what this wine represented better than keeping it in a dark room?"

"He's right," Brix murmured.

"The decision is not one to be made lightly." Tryst turned to me. "Or without the Hopes' consent."

The only way to help Saffron and her family was to admit I knew her reason for wanting to make the wine. Something she'd likely see as a betrayal. It also meant her father would need to know what she intended to do.

"Let it serve as a backup plan for now," Cru suggested. "If we can't find Concepción's notes, we'd at least have this."

I looked around the circle. "I'm asking for a lot. Your time, your labor, your discretion. And potentially, this bottle. But I know this will be worth it."

"We need to vote," Brix said. "All in favor of granting this brotherhood's resources to pull this together in any way possible, raise your hand."

It was more than I'd asked, and I wondered if anyone would challenge my brother. However, every hand went up. There wasn't a single dissent.

Two hurdles were crossed. My family had agreed to help, as did Los Caballeros. Now, the real work—and struggle—would begin.

The meeting broke up with the usual protocols—handshakes, quiet conversations, plans being made. I stayed near the table, fielding questions from the *Viejos* about timing and logistics until most of them had filtered out.

I noticed Kick waiting near the stone wall. When I made my way over, he fell into step beside me as we headed out of the caves.

"That was intense," he said.

"Yeah."

"Tryst offering up that bottle—didn't see that coming."

I glanced at him. "You think we should use it?"

"I think we should find Concepción's notes first." He kicked at a loose rock on the path. "But if it comes down to analyzing that bottle or watching the Hopes lose everything? Then yeah, we use it."

We walked in silence for a few more steps before he spoke again. "You know what you're getting yourself into with all this?"

"Making wine? I've done it before."

"Not what I meant, and you know it."

I stopped walking and faced him. "I don't."

"You're about to spend the next six weeks working side by side with Saffron Hope. Every day. Long hours. Close quarters." He raised a brow. "You sure you can handle that without making things complicated?"

"Things are already complicated."

"Yeah, but right now, in a way you can ignore. Once you're in the thick of this—harvest, fermentation, bottling—you won't be able to ignore anything."

He wasn't wrong. "What would you do?"

Kick's expression was unreadable, and he was quiet for a moment. "Honestly? I'd tell her how I felt before we got started. Get it out in the open so there's no question about where you stand."

"That's a terrible idea."

"Probably." He grinned. "But at least then you'd know if she feels the same way before you spend six weeks torturing yourself."

"She doesn't."

"You sure about that?"

I thought about the way she'd looked at me across the table at the diner. The tears in her eyes when I'd promised to help. The way she'd squeezed my hand like I was the only solid thing in her world. "No. I'm not sure about anything when it comes to her."

"Then maybe it's time to find out." He clapped me on the shoulder. "Either way, you've got my help as well as the rest of the *caballeros*. Whatever you need—crew, equipment, someone to kick your ass when you're being an idiot—I'm here."

"Thanks, man."

We reached our trucks, and he paused with his hand on the door handle. "One more thing."

"What?"

"Don't overthink this. You've got a tendency to get in your own head and talk yourself out of the good shit." His expression turned serious. "Don't let Saffron slip away because you're too scared to take the shot, Snap."

I nodded.

"So what will you tell her?" he asked.

"Fuck if I know," I said honestly.

He squeezed my shoulder. "I wish I could offer words of wisdom."

"Me too." But no one could. I just prayed that whatever I came up with, she'd believe.

5

Snapper

It was midafternoon but still warm for this time of year as I drove to Saffron's house. The Hope Family Winery property sat on a hill overlooking the valley. The main house was a sprawling craftsman-style home that had been in her family for three generations. I'd been here dozens of times over the years—for parties, tastings, casual visits. But today felt different. Today, I was bringing her hope.

I parked in the circular driveway and climbed the front steps. Before I could knock, the door swung open.

Saffron stood there in the same jeans and flannel shirt she'd worn at breakfast. Now, though, her hair was up in a ponytail, her makeup was no longer apparent, and her feet were bare. She looked exhausted and beautiful and so damn vulnerable it made my chest ache.

"Snapper. I didn't expect—did you—" It was as though whatever she wanted to say got stuck in her throat.

"Can I come in?"

"Of course. Sorry." She stepped to the side to let me pass.

The house was quiet. "Are your parents home?"

"No, they left this morning for Napa with Felicity and Wagner. The baby is due any day now."

"How long will they be gone?" I asked, relieved I didn't have to tell her what transpired since we left the diner in front of them.

"No idea." She wrapped her arms around herself. "Why? Did you—did you talk to your brothers and Alex?"

"I did."

Her face went pale. "And?"

I let myself smile. "They're in. All of them. We're doing this, Saffron."

For a second, she just stared at me. Then her hands flew to her mouth, and tears she tried to blink away filled her eyes. "Really? You're serious?"

"Completely." I stepped closer. "Cru confirmed we have the grapes you need. The Syrah will be ready in about a week, the Gamay in two. If your Zinfandel is ready sooner, we can start there."

"It might be. I haven't checked since Friday, but—" She broke off, laughing.

I wanted to pull her into my arms, but kept my hands at my sides. "We'll check all three varietals tomorrow at dawn. Walk your vineyards first, then ours. See what we're working with."

"Thank you. I don't even know what to say."

"You don't have to thank me. We're partners, remember? Fifty-fifty."

She smiled, and it transformed her whole face. "Still, thanks."

"There is something we could do in the meantime," I said.

"What's that?"

"Look for Concepción's notes. You checked your attic. We should check my ma's." I paused. "Want to help? We've got a couple hours of daylight left."

She glanced toward the stairs, then back at me. "I should probably shower first. I'm a mess."

"You look fine." More than fine, but I wasn't about to say that.

"Give me fifteen minutes. I'll change and meet you there."

"I'll be waiting."

I watched her run up the stairs, then let myself out.

Twenty minutes later, Saffron arrived at the main house at Los Cab, where I'd been waiting outside for her. She'd changed into fitted jeans and a soft gray Henley that hugged her curves in ways that made my mouth go dry. Her hair was still damp from the shower, falling in waves past her shoulders.

"Sorry I'm late," she said, climbing out of her truck. "I couldn't find my good flashlight."

"We won't need it. The attic has lights." I hoped. "Come on."

My mother was in the kitchen when we walked in, and the smell of cinnamon filled the air.

"Salazar? Is that you?" she called.

"Yeah, Ma. I brought Saffron."

My mom appeared in the hallway, wiping her hands on a dish towel. "*Mija!* What a wonderful surprise."

"Hi, Mrs. Avila." Saffron's smile lit up the room—and my heart, if I was honest. "Sorry to drop in unannounced."

"Don't be silly. You're always welcome here." Ma hugged her, then leaned away. "Are you eating enough? You look too thin."

"She ate fine this morning," I muttered. "All *my* food, in fact."

Saffron elbowed me. "He's right. I did eat most of his breakfast. You should worry more about him."

My mother made a noncommittal sound. "I have snickerdoodles cooling on the counter. Fresh out of the oven."

"Actually, we need to look through the attic. We're searching for some old family records."

"The attic?" One brow rose. "What kind of records?"

"Anything from Eduardo and Concepción's time. We're looking for wine formulas."

"For the Christmas Blessing Wine?" Ma's eyes widened.

I was stunned she knew about it and said so.

"Of course I know about it. You're going to make it?"

"We're going to try," Saffron said.

"That's wonderful." Ma pressed a hand to her chest. "You're welcome to check the attic if you want, but I don't remember seeing anything like that."

"Thanks, Ma."

"I'll give you some cookies to take up with you," she said, already heading back to the kitchen.

After grabbing a platter of snickerdoodles that my mom had covered with plastic wrap—good thinking—I led Saffron upstairs and pulled the attic ladder down. It groaned in protest, raining dust on both of us.

"Watch your step," I said, climbing up first. "The boards creak."

The attic was exactly as I remembered—cramped, hot, and packed with decades of accumulated family history. I found the light switch, and three of the four bulbs flickered to life, casting weak yellow light over the space.

Saffron climbed up behind me. "This looks just like ours."

"Three generations of pack rats will do that." I surveyed the stacks of boxes and trunks. "Where should we start?"

"The oldest-looking stuff?" She pointed toward a section near the window, where several steamer trunks sat.

The floorboards groaned under our weight as we made our way over. The attic was stifling. I could already feel sweat forming at the base of my spine.

The first trunk we opened held baby clothes—tiny gowns and knitted booties that probably belonged to my siblings or me. The second had photo albums, their pages yellowed with age.

"Look at this," Saffron said, opening another trunk and removing a wedding dress that I knew hadn't belonged to my mom. Maybe my grandmother. She sighed. "It's so beautiful."

I moved behind her to look over her shoulder. The citrusy and sweet scent of her shampoo hit me, making me want to bury my face in her hair. My chest brushed against her back, and I felt her go still.

"Sorry," I said, not moving away. "Tight quarters up here."

"It's fine."

It wasn't fine. Being this close to her, feeling the warmth of her body through our clothes, breathing her in—my brain was short-circuiting. I let my breath ghost across the back of her neck before forcing myself to step away.

She carefully set the dress aside and dug deeper. Under it were more clothes, a rosary, and a small wooden box with initials carved into the lid.

"EA," she read. "Eduardo Avila?"

"Probably." I opened another trunk nearby while she explored the box. Inside were old receipts, tax documents, and letters tied with string. But nothing that looked like wine formulas.

Heat built steadily in the enclosed space, and sweat trickled down my spine as we worked in silence.

Eventually, I gave in and removed my flannel, leaving just my undershirt. The cooler air against my skin helped marginally.

When I glanced over and our eyes met, she quickly looked away, but not before I caught the flush creeping up her neck.

Interesting.

"Find anything?" I asked.

"Nothing about wine." She sounded flustered.

I reached for another box at the same moment she did. Our fingers touched, and she jerked her hand away. "You get this one. I'll check over there," she said.

When I opened it, I found more photographs, but instead of in albums, these were loose. I flipped through them slowly. Most were of people I didn't recognize. Then I found one that made me pause. Two women standing in front of old wooden fermentation tanks. On the back, someone had written, "Mar and Connie, 1954."

"Saffron, check this out."

She came closer, looking over my shoulder, and I had to concentrate on slowing my breathing. "That's my great-grandmother. Marilyn."

"With my great-grandmother, Concepción." I pointed to the second woman. Behind them, partially out of frame, was a third figure. "There's someone else with them."

Her breast pressed against my arm when she bent closer. I didn't think she even noticed, but I sure as hell did. "It's hard to see who it is. Not that I'd know who they were even if I could."

"Nothing written on the back." I flipped through more photos. "Wait, here's another one."

This one showed three women together, all smiling at the camera. Marilyn and Concepción were clearly identifiable. The third woman was tall and elegant, with striking features.

"Who is she?" Saffron murmured.

"I don't know. But she's in several of these." I showed her three more photos, each featuring the mystery woman with various combinations of family members.

Only one had a name on the back. *Ellen.*

"Ellen who, though?" I mumbled.

"Good question." Saffron wiped sweat from her temple.

"Yeah." I was acutely aware of her proximity, the way her shirt was starting to stick to her skin, the damp tendrils of hair curling at her neck. "We can take a break if you want."

"No, let's keep going. We're running out of daylight."

We searched for another thirty minutes but found nothing that looked like wine formulas or technical notes. Just photographs, letters, and other personal effects. Rather than cooling off, the heat was becoming unbearable.

"I need some air," Saffron said, fanning herself.

"Same. Let's go downstairs."

I climbed down the ladder first, then waited at the bottom to help her. She was midway when her foot slipped on the dusty rung.

"Careful!" I grabbed her waist to steady her, then turned her in my arms.

She gripped my shoulders, and we froze like that, our faces a couple of inches apart, my hands on her waist, and her body pressed against mine.

"Thanks," she whispered.

"Anytime." I should've let go, but couldn't bring myself to.

Her eyes dropped to my mouth, then her gaze returned to mine. All I had to do was close that small distance, and—

"What are you doing up there? Dinner's almost ready!" Ma hollered from the kitchen.

Saffron jerked away and practically jumped the rest of the way down the ladder.

"We should…" She gestured toward the stairs.

"Yeah."

We found Ma in the kitchen, checking something in the oven. She took one look at us—both flushed and disheveled—and her knowing smile made me want to sink into the floor.

"Find anything interesting?" she asked, wriggling her eyebrows.

"Just some photos," I managed.

"Well, you're welcome to keep looking. But first, eat." She pushed a basket containing warm rolls in our direction.

Saffron took one and bit into it. "Oh my God, these are amazing."

"Have as many as you want, *mija*. You need meat on your bones."

I grabbed three myself and rested against the counter, watching Saffron eat. She had a smudge of dirt on her cheek from the attic, and her hair was falling out of its ponytail, but she still looked so beautiful that she took my breath away.

"You have something…" I reached out and wiped the smudge away with my thumb.

She went very still. "Thanks."

"Anytime." I let my thumb linger maybe a second too long before lowering my hand.

Ma watched this exchange with barely concealed delight. "You know, there are more places to look for those formulas. The old winery building. The caves."

"That's right. The caves have a records room," I said. "We could check there."

"Now?" Saffron glanced out the window. The sun was low on the horizon.

"We've got lights."

"Okay. Let's try," she said after hesitating for a few seconds.

"Dinner is at seven," my mother reminded me. "Don't be late."

"I won't, Ma." I kissed her cheek and motioned Saffron in the direction of the door to the porch.

Outside, the evening air felt blessedly cool after the attic as we walked the path toward the caves' entrance.

"Your mom is wonderful," Saffron said.

"She likes you."

"How can you tell?"

"She gave you cookies and rolls. Ma only shares those with really special people."

Saffron smiled. "I'm honored."

"You should be. Kick's been trying to get on her good side for twenty-eight years. Still hasn't managed it."

She laughed, and the sound made my chest warm.

"Cold?" I asked when we walked in and she shivered and rubbed her arms.

"Yes, but I'll adjust."

I led her farther in, past barrel rooms filled with aging wine, through passages carved into the hillside decades ago. The records room, a small chamber lined with filing cabinets and boxes, was in the east branch.

"This is going to take forever," Saffron said, surveying the sheer volume of material.

"Then, we better get started." I grabbed a bottle of Zinfandel from a nearby rack. "Want some?"

"We're working."

"We can work and drink." I found wineglasses on a shelf and poured. "It'll make the time go faster."

She accepted the glass and took a sip, her eyes closing briefly.

We settled on the stone floor and started going through the boxes. While we found notes about various vintages, most were recent. I couldn't help glancing at her every few seconds—the way she concentrated, the furrow between her brows, the way she tucked her hair behind her ear repeatedly.

"Why are you staring at me?" she asked without looking up.

"I'm not."

"You are."

"Can't a guy appreciate a pretty woman?"

She raised a brow. "Are you flirting with me?"

"Maybe. Is it working?"

"No." But her mouth curved up at the corners, betraying her.

"Liar."

She shook her head and reached for another box, but that ghost of a smile lingered.

"How come we never…?" I started, then stopped.

"Never what?"

"You know. You and me."

She froze, her hand halfway into a box. "What?"

"We've known each other for years. We're friends. But how come we never tried to be more?"

Her expression shuttered. "It wasn't worth the risk."

"You never know until you try."

"Snapper—"

"I'm serious. What if—"

"You're just bored," she cut me off. "No rodeo this year means no buckle bunnies throwing themselves at you. I'm convenient. That's all."

That stung. "Is that really what you think?"

"It's not like you're ever around anyway." She sorted through a stack of papers without meeting my eyes. "And when you are, you turn right around and leave again."

"I'm here now."

"For how long? Until your shoulder heals and you're back on the circuit?"

Fair question. One I didn't have a good response for. "Saffron—"

"Let's just keep looking, okay?" She turned away, shutting down the conversation.

I wanted to push. Wanted to tell her she was wrong, that she wasn't convenient, that I'd been half in love with her for years. But the set of her shoulders told me now wasn't the time.

We searched in silence for another hour. I found old correspondence, barrel inventories, nothing useful. Then Saffron gasped.

"What?" I moved closer.

She held up a leather-bound journal, smaller than Marilyn's but similar in style. "Look at the inside cover."

I leaned in to read the faded inscription: "Concepción Maria Ramirez Avila."

"Holy shit."

She carefully turned pages filled with flowing handwriting. Some entries were in English, others in Spanish. There were recipes, family notes, and daily observations. Then she stopped on an entry dated February 1956.

"Listen to this," she said, reading aloud. "'My heart is breaking. E says she won't allow us to make the wine again. M and I have agreed—I will keep my formulas; she will keep hers. What we created together is finished.'"

"'She won't allow,'" I repeated. "E is a woman."

"Ellen," Saffron said, looking at the photograph of the three women. "E is Ellen."

"But who was she? And what did she do?" I shook my head. "We need to figure out who she is."

Saffron continued reading, but the entries became less specific after that. Just daily observations and recipes.

"This doesn't help us much," she said, closing the journal. "We still don't have the formulas we need. At least not the percentages."

"On the other hand, we know we're on the right track." I stood and offered her my hand. "Come on. It's getting late."

She let me pull her up, and for a moment, we stood there, hands linked, close enough that I could see the flecks of gold in her eyes.

"Thank you," she said quietly. "For today. For everything."

"We're partners, remember?"

She squeezed my hand once before letting go. "Is that what we are?"

I took a step forward and reached for her. "Saffron, I—"

"I can't do this."

Before I realized what was happening, she sprinted from the records room. I raced after her.

"Saffron, wait!" I shouted when I saw her head out the main entrance.

"I need to get home," she said over her shoulder when I caught up with her. By then we were halfway to her truck.

I stopped running and put my hands on my hips. "I thought you were staying for dinner."

She stopped too and turned to look at me. "I'm grungy from being in attics and caves all day. Thank your mom for me."

"Thank her yourself," I muttered when she took off again. This time, I didn't try to catch her.

Kick stood near the table, beer in hand, talking to Cru about something related to the vineyard blocks. When he saw me, he raised his bottle in greeting.

"Where's Saffron?" he asked. "Ma said she was with you."

"She left."

His eyebrows rose. "What happened?"

I shook my head, not wanting to get into it here, with half the family within earshot.

He stood and jerked his head toward the porch. I followed him outside, where the evening air had turned cool.

"Talk," he said once we were alone.

"Nothing happened. We were looking for Concepción's notes in the caves, found her journal, and then Saffron just bolted."

"Did you say something?"

"I tried to." I held onto the porch rail. "She wouldn't let me."

"You know what your problem is?"

"I'm sure you're about to tell me."

He set his beer down. "She's drowning right now, Snap. Her family's about to lose everything, and you're standing there asking her to figure out what you two are to each other."

"Wait a minute. Aren't you the guy who told me to tell her how I felt upfront? If I remember correctly, you said I should get it out in the open so there's no question about where I stand."

"You, Snap. Not her. *You.*"

I looked up at the sky. "I'm lost."

"There's a difference between saying, 'Hey, Saffron, I'm crazy about you, and whatever you need, I'm your guy,' and forcing her to think about things she doesn't have the brain space to deal with right now."

"I wasn't forcing anything—"

"Yeah, you were. I know you." He crossed his arms. "You want to fix everything at once. Help her with the wine, get her to admit she has feelings for you, all while she's trying to keep her head above water."

The accuracy of that hit harder than I wanted to admit.

"So what do I do?"

"What you said you'd do, and let everything else happen when it happens. Be honest with her about how *you* feel." He picked up his beer again. "She'll come around. But she's gotta do it on her own timeline, not yours."

"And if she doesn't?"

"She will." He clapped me on the shoulder. "I know it."

We headed back inside, and I wanted to ask him how he could be so certain, but Ma was calling everyone to the table.

"Where's Saffron?" she asked like Kick had.

"She had to go home."

"That's too bad. I was hoping she'd stay."

Me too.

Dinner was the usual chaos—too many people talking at once, Reagan and Neva demanding attention, Bit and Cru arguing about some vintage they'd tried last week. I picked at my food and contributed when someone asked me a direct question, but mostly, I just sat there, thinking about the woman I came so close to kissing.

"What did Saffron say about opening the bottle of Christmas Blessing Wine Tryst found?" Bit asked.

I hung my head and shook it. I'd completely forgotten to bring it up. Where in the hell had my head been? That was a stupid question. On her. All on her.

"Don't give up on her," Bit said, squeezing my shoulder and looking at me as though he could read my thoughts.

"No? You should've seen her—"

"I did."

"Leaving?" I asked.

"Yep."

"So then, you know. She wants nothing to do with me."

He took my arm and led me outside. "You're wrong. So wrong."

"Yeah? If that's the case, how do you explain why she had to get away from me like her life depended on it?"

"Because it does."

"Bit—"

"Hear me out. She's scared."

"Of what?"

"Of needing you." Bit swirled wine in the glass I hadn't realized he brought out with him. I grabbed it and took a swig, remembering I had to return to the caves to put the stuff away we'd left out, and that included the bottle of Zin I'd opened.

"What's so bad about needing me?" I asked.

"What happens if she lets herself and you leave?"

"I'm not going anywhere."

"Does she know that?" His eyes met mine. "Or does she just know you as the guy who's gone most of the year chasing rodeo championships? The guy who's never settled down, never committed to anything but the next ride?"

His words hit hard, but that was Bit, I reminded myself. He told it like he saw it. "That's not fair."

"Isn't it?" His tone was gentle. "You've been running from this place, from the family business, from putting down roots, for years. She has no reason to believe you'd stay."

"But I would."

"Then, prove it." He put his hand on my shoulder again. "Keep showing up. Keep helping. Don't push for more than she can give right now."

"And if that doesn't work?"

"I told you before. I'd do everything humanly possible for the woman I love. In fact, I did. You should too."

6

Saffron

I made it halfway home before the tears started.

What the hell was wrong with me? Snapper had been about to—what? Kiss me? Tell me something important? And I'd run like a scared rabbit.

The steering wheel was slick under my palms as I gripped it tighter, trying to focus on the dark road ahead instead of the memory of standing so close to him in the caves. The way his eyes had searched mine. The warmth of his body so close to mine. That moment when everything had hung, suspended between us.

"We're partners, remember?" he'd said.

"Is that what we are?" I'd whispered back.

Then he'd stepped closer, reached for me, and I'd panicked.

By the time I drove through our front gate, my hands were shaking. The house loomed dark and empty with my parents gone.

I climbed out of my truck and stood in the cool evening air, staring up at the winery buildings silhouetted against the darkening sky.

And I'd just run away from the one person willing to help us. Help me.

Inside, the house was eerily still. I kicked off my shoes, dropped my purse on the counter, and stood in the kitchen, trying to figure out what to do next. Call him? Apologize? Explain?

Explain what? That I was terrified? That every time he got close, I wanted him so badly I could barely breathe? That I'd been in love with him for so long I didn't know how not to be?

Yeah, that would go over well.

I was pulling a bottle of wine from the rack—screw it, I needed a drink—when headlights swept across the kitchen window.

My heart leaped. Snapper. He'd followed me home to—

But when I looked out, I saw a sleek Mercedes, not Snapper's truck.

Jesus. It was Isabel Van Orr. What the hell was she doing here?

I set the wine bottle down and went to the door, opening it before she could knock.

"This is unexpected."

She stood on my porch in designer jeans and cashmere, her blonde hair perfect even at this hour, diamonds glinting at her ears and throat, and as usual, her smile was ice cold.

"I hope I'm not intruding. I was hoping we could talk. You know, woman to woman."

Every instinct screamed at me to say no, to close the door. Instead, I stepped aside and waved her in.

She walked past me into the kitchen, her expensive perfume trailing behind her. Her gaze swept the room—taking in the wine bottle I'd left on the counter before looking me up and down.

"What did you want to talk to me about?" I asked, not bothering to hide the edge in my voice.

"I wanted to warn you. About Snapper."

My stomach twisted. "Warn me about what?"

"You've always been a bit naive, Saffron. I'd hate to see you get hurt." She tilted her head, contemplating me like I was something under a microscope. "You bid seventy-five thousand dollars on him last night. That's just sad, sweetheart. And desperate."

"That's none of your business."

"Maybe not. But I've known Snapper a long time. Maybe not longer than you but more intimately, if you know what I mean. So, unlike you, I know what kind of man he really is."

"Is that so? What kind of man is he?"

She moved closer. "The kind who'll fuck you and leave you. In fact, I heard him say, 'Fuck 'em and leave 'em.' to his brothers."

I hugged my arms around myself tighter. "I don't believe you."

"That's your choice." She shrugged. "But ask yourself—why is he suddenly so interested in you now? After all these years of keeping you in the friend zone?"

Because I asked for help. Because I need him. The thoughts whispered through my mind, poisonous and insidious.

"You're convenient," Isabel continued. "His shoulder's injured, so he's not on the rodeo circuit this year. No buckle bunnies throwing themselves at him. You're here. You're available. And you're clearly willing."

"Get out." I shook with anger I was trying hard to control.

"I'm just trying to help you, Saffron. Save you from making a fool of yourself." She paused, examining her manicured nails. "Though I suppose you wouldn't be the first woman in your family to fall for his charms."

"What are you talking about?"

"Oh, you didn't know?" Her smile sharpened. "About Felicity and Snapper? I always thought you and your sister were close."

The room tilted. "You're lying."

"Am I? Ask her yourself." Isabel moved toward the door, then paused. "It was years ago, of course. Before Wagner. But once was enough for your sister to know what kind of man he really is. She could warn you, if you were brave enough to ask. You know—*woman to woman*."

Then she was gone, her taillights disappearing down the driveway.

I stood frozen in my kitchen as Isabel's accusations echoed in my head.

Fuck 'em and leave 'em.

Felicity and Snapper.

No, that couldn't be right. Felicity would have told me. We told each other everything. And Snapper wasn't—he wouldn't—

Except what did I really know about his romantic life? He was gone ten months a year. Who knew what he did on the rodeo circuit? And when had he ever looked at me as anything more than a friend?

Until today.

Until that moment in the caves when he'd reached for me and I'd seen something in his eyes that made my heart race and my stomach flip and every nerve ending in my body come alive.

You're convenient.

God, what if she was right?

I grabbed the wine bottle and poured myself a generous glass. I needed to call Felicity. Needed to ask her—but I couldn't. Not now. Not when she was about to go into labor any second.

But Isabel's story ate at me. Was she right? Had something happened between Felicity and Snapper? When? During one of Snapper's rare trips home? How long ago?

The mental images running through my head made bile rise in my throat.

I was halfway through my second glass of wine when I heard another vehicle in the driveway.

This time, it was Snapper's truck.

I wasn't ready to face him with Isabel's poison still fresh in my mind.

But he was already climbing out, already heading for the porch. And he was carrying something wrapped in cloth.

I opened the door before he could knock.

"Hey," he said.

"Hey."

His expression shifted to concern. "You okay?"

"Fine."

"You sure? Because you look—" He stopped. "Can I come in?"

I stepped aside to let him pass, just like I had my last *visitor*. He moved into the kitchen and carefully set whatever he was carrying on the counter.

"What's that?" I asked.

"Something I need to show you." He unwrapped the cloth that covered a wine bottle. It was old, dusty, and the label was faded but still legible—Christmas Blessing Wine, 1955.

"Oh my God." I moved closer, my hands hovering near it but not quite touching. "Where did you find this?"

"In the rare room. In the caves." He watched my reaction. "After you left, I went back to the house, and Bit reminded me that Tryst had found it."

I stared at the bottle, my mind racing. "There's actually a bottle. A real bottle."

"Just one, as far as we know."

"This is incredible." I reached out, then stopped myself.

"We could have it analyzed," Snapper said. "Modern technology can determine the exact composition. We wouldn't need to find the missing formulas. We'd have everything we need."

"Really? That's possible?"

"Yeah. But, Saffron...Once we open it, it's gone. Opening it means destroying it forever."

"We can't."

"It might be our only option—"

"No." I stepped away from the counter, from the bottle, from him. "This is part of your family's history. Part of mine too. Once it's poured down some lab drain, it's gone. We can't undo that."

"But then we'd have the formula—"

"Maybe. What if the technology isn't perfect? What if it can't capture exactly what they did? What if there's some step, some technique that isn't in the chemistry of the wine itself? I can't be responsible for destroying the only evidence that this wine ever existed."

He moved closer. "Saffron, listen to me—"

"No." I held up a hand. "You listen. I appreciate that you found it. I appreciate that your family agreed to help. But I can't—I won't—destroy something this important on the chance that maybe it'll give us what we need."

"Even if it could save you?"

His statement hung in the air between us, heavy with implication.

My throat closed. "What do you mean?"

He searched my face. "I know something's wrong. Something big. And you won't tell me what it is."

"I don't know what you're talking about."

"Yes, you do." He took another step closer. "I've known you too long. I can see it in your face, in the way you can barely hold it together. The desperation. The fear. Dammit, Saffron, why won't you just tell me?"

"There's nothing—"

"Stop lying to me!" His frustration nearly undid me. "You *know* I'll help. But you have to fucking trust me."

Tears burned behind my eyes and I shook my head.

"Why can't you tell me?"

Because you'll offer money. Because my father will refuse. Because you'll leave anyway, and I'll be left with nothing but a broken heart and a foreclosed winery.

Because Isabel was right—I'm just convenient.

"Saffron." He stepped close enough that I could feel the warmth radiating off his body. "Talk to me. *Please.*"

I shook my head, unable to speak.

His hand came up, cupping my face with a gentleness that made everything inside me crack. "Why won't you let me in?"

"Because—" I couldn't continue.

His thumb caught a tear I hadn't realized had fallen. "What are you afraid of?"

"That you'll leave. That I don't matter." It all poured out of me, years of frustration and longing spilling over. "I'm convenient. Available. And—"

His other hand came up to frame my face. "You think that's all you are to me? Convenient?"

"Aren't I?"

"No." His tone was fierce. "You're not convenient. You've never been convenient. You've been—" He stopped, and his eyes searched mine. "You've been the one person I couldn't stop thinking about. The one person I looked forward to seeing every time I came home. The reason I started coming home more often even when I didn't need to."

"Snapper—"

"How can you not know how I feel about you?" The question came out raw and honest. "I care about you. Not because you're convenient or available or any of that bullshit. Because you're you. Because you're smart and stubborn and you call me out on my shit. Because you make me want to be a better man. Because when you smile at me, really smile, it feels like the warmest sun is shining on me."

I couldn't breathe. Couldn't think. All I could do was stare at him as what he'd said rewrote everything I thought I knew.

"I'm done keeping my distance," he continued. "Done waiting for you to catch up. So I'm telling you now—you matter to me. More than you know."

"I don't—I can't—"

He shifted closer, his forehead nearly touching mine. "Tell me you don't feel it too. Tell me I'm alone in this, and I'll back off. But if there's any chance you feel even a fraction of what I do—"

I kissed him.

Or he kissed me.

I wasn't sure who moved first, only that his mouth was on mine and everything else disappeared.

His lips were warm, firm, and perfect. His fingers weaved into my hair, tilting my head back, deepening the kiss. The other moved to my waist, pulling me closer, and I went willingly, pressing against him like I could melt into his body.

He kissed me like he'd been starving for it. Like I was air and he'd been drowning. His tongue swept into my mouth, and I gasped, the sound swallowed by his lips.

He moved us until my back hit the wall, his body pinning me there. His thigh pushed between mine, and I whimpered into his mouth. The sound seemed to break something in him because his kiss went from desperate to consuming.

His hand slid from my waist to my hip, then lower, gripping my thigh and hitching it up around his waist. The new angle pressed us together more intimately, and I could feel how much he wanted this. Wanted me.

"Saffron." My name against my mouth was rough and reverent.

I kissed him again, harder, trying to show him with my body what I couldn't say. That I'd wanted this for so long. That he'd been right—I did feel it too. More than a fraction. All of it.

His mouth moved to my neck, and I tilted my head back, giving him access. His teeth grazed my pulse point, and my nails dug into his shoulders.

"Tell me," he breathed against my skin. "Tell me you feel this."

"I feel it." The admission came out broken. "I feel it so much I can't breathe."

His chest heaved against me, both of us breathing hard. "Then, tell me the truth. Tell me what's really going on. Let me help you."

His words were like being doused with cold water.

Reality crashed back in. The foreclosure. The fact that wanting him and trusting him were two different things.

"I can't."

His expression shifted—hurt, then frustrated, then angry. "Can't or won't?"

"Does it matter?"

"Yeah, it does." He stepped away, putting space between us that felt like a chasm. "Because I just laid everything out there. Told you how I feel. Kissed you like—" He stopped, running a hand through his hair. "And you still can't confide in me."

"Snapper—"

"No." He held up a hand. "I get it. You're scared. Fine. But I can't—" His jaw clenched. "I can't do this halfway. I can't kiss you like that and act like everything's okay when you can't even be honest with me."

Tears spilled down my cheeks. "I don't know how."

"Then, figure it out." He spoke gently but firmly. "Because whatever this is between us—it only works if you talk to me. Not just about the easy stuff, but with the hard stuff too."

He moved to the counter and carefully wrapped the bottle back in its cloth. Then he looked at me one more time, his eyes holding mine.

"I meant what I said. You matter to me. More than anything or anyone. I meant that. But you have to let me in, Saffron. All the way in. Not just the parts you think are safe."

Then he was gone.

The door closed behind him, and I slid down the wall. I sat on the kitchen floor, hugging my knees to my chest as sobs wracked my body.

He was right. I knew he was right.

But what Isabel said still echoed in my head. And I didn't know how to reconcile the man who'd just kissed me like I was precious with the one who supposedly said "fuck 'em and leave 'em." Not to mention the possibility that I wasn't the first Hope girl he'd kissed. I shuddered. I couldn't think about him and my sister now. My focus had to remain on figuring out how to make the wine I prayed would save our family. But I didn't know how to accept that he'd stay when he never had before.

And I didn't know how to tell him the truth when admitting it meant showing him just how badly we were failing. How desperate I really was.

My phone buzzed on the counter above me. I reached up blindly, grabbed it, and read Snapper's message.

I'm not giving up on you. Or us. Or this wine. But you have to meet me halfway. Please. I'll be there at sunup, and we'll walk the vineyard.

Fresh tears blurred my vision as I responded, *Okay*.

It wasn't much. But it was all I had to give right now.

Before I could set the phone down, it buzzed again with a text from Felicity.

My back is KILLING me, and I've had Braxton Hicks all day. Doctor says could be any day now. You're coming, right? The second I go into labor?

My stomach twisted. *Of course. I promised, didn't I?*

You better. I can't do this without my sister. Love you!

Love you too, and see you and that little one SOON!

I set the phone down and stared at the ceiling.

What if Felicity went into labor in the next week? What if I had to choose between being there for the birth of my niece or nephew and being here to save our family's winery?

What if the two most important things in my life happened at the exact same time and I could only choose one?

The thought made me want to throw up.

I opened my calendar app. Felicity's actual due date was eight days away.

The Zinfandel would be ready in two to three days. The Syrah would follow about a week later, and the Gamay would be last.

If the baby was late, I could make it work. Be at all three harvests and still get to Napa before he or she came.

If she went into labor early—or even on time—I couldn't finish the thought.

My phone buzzed again with another message from Snapper.

Stop overthinking. You'll figure it out. You always do. Now GO TO SLEEP.

I smiled through fresh tears and set the phone down again.

But sleep didn't come for a long time.

7

Snapper

Every inch of me ached. Not just my rock-hard cock, but my hands that were no longer on Saffron's body. My lips and tongue that were starved for her. And my heart, because I wanted her to tell me what I already knew and, for some reason, she couldn't bring herself to admit to me. That nearly crushed me. If she didn't believe in me enough to tell me her family was in trouble, then I couldn't trust that intimacy between us would matter as much to her as it would to me.

The worst part was knowing she wanted me. The kiss proved that. The way she'd melted against me, the way she'd kissed me back like her life depended on it—that wasn't fake. But the second I'd asked for truth, for her to let me in past those walls she kept so high, she'd rebuilt them brick by brick right in front of me.

I parked my truck in front of the main house and sat in the darkness while the engine ticked as it cooled.

The photo we'd found earlier—the one with Marilyn, Concepción, and the mystery Ellen woman—sat on the passenger seat where I'd tossed it after leaving Saffron's. I picked it up and viewed it again under the dome light, as if staring at it long enough would reveal who this woman was and what role she'd played in destroying the wine collaboration.

I looked up at the mostly dark windows. Sunday dinner had ended hours ago, and everyone had gone home or to bed. I should do the same. Head to my place in Paso Robles, get some sleep, and figure out what the hell to do tomorrow.

But I couldn't make myself move. I couldn't stop tasting her on my lips or feeling the phantom touch of her hands in my hair.

The kitchen light was still on, which surprised me at almost eleven on a Sunday night. I grabbed the photo and went inside.

"Back already?" Tryst asked when I found him sitting at the counter. "I thought you'd be gone longer." He took one look at my face, and his expression shifted. "What happened?"

"She won't do it." I dropped onto the stool across from him. "I showed her the bottle, explained we could have it analyzed and get everything we need. She refused."

"Because?"

"She says it's too important. Part of both our families' histories. That we can't destroy the only evidence the wine ever existed." I ran a hand through my hair. "She's not wrong. But without the formula…"

"You'll find it," said Tryst with certainty. "You have time."

"Do we?" My response came out harsher than I intended. "I don't know how much time we actually have."

Tryst moved to the cabinet and reached for two rocks glasses and the bottle of whiskey bottle he knew was kept on the top shelf. He poured two generous measures and passed one over to me.

I took a drink and welcomed the burn.

"What else happened tonight?" he asked.

Everything. Nothing. I kissed her, and she kissed me back, and then she shut down the second I asked her to confide in me.

But I couldn't say that. Not yet.

Instead, I took the photo out of my pocket and set it on the counter. "We found this. Three women—Marilyn Hope, Concepción Avila, and someone identified only as Ellen on the back."

Tryst picked up the photo and angled it toward the light. His brow furrowed. "Ellen," he murmured. "I don't recognize her."

"Neither do we. But according to Concepción's journal, E, who we've determined is Ellen, wouldn't *allow* them to make the wine again."

"And you think she held part of the formula."

"Maybe. She obviously had something to do with it, or they would've made it again the following year on their own." I took another drink.

Tryst continued studying the photo, then shook his head. "I don't know her. But some of the other *Viejos* might. Men whose fathers were making wine in 1955— they might have heard stories, seen photos."

Hope flickered in my chest. "You think so?"

"It's worth asking." He set the photo down carefully. "I'll make some calls tomorrow. See what I can dig up."

"Thank you."

He refilled both our glasses even though mine wasn't quite empty. "You look exhausted, Salazar. You have an early morning tomorrow—walking the vineyards with Saffron at dawn, yes?"

"I am."

"Then, go home. Get some rest. This will still be here in the morning, and you'll need your wits about you."

He was right. I was running on fumes and emotion, neither of which would help me tomorrow.

I finished my whiskey, pocketed the photo, and stood. "Thanks, *Tío*."

"De nada, mijo." He squeezed my shoulder. "And, Salazar? Don't give up on her. She's worth fighting for."

My throat tightened. "I know she is."

The drive to my house took fifteen minutes through dark, winding roads. When I turned onto my street, I immediately noticed that Kick's place was lit up, and there was a car in his driveway.

I slowed as I passed, trying to get a better look at the vehicle. It was small, dark-colored—a sedan maybe. The same kind of car I'd seen leaving Saffron's driveway earlier tonight when I'd arrived.

Was it the same? I couldn't be sure in the darkness. And even if it was, what did that mean? That Saffron's "friend from town" was now at Kick's place?

None of my business, I reminded myself. Kick's personal life was his own.

But the coincidence nagged at me as I arrived at my house and parked in the garage.

My house in Paso Robles sat on three acres just outside downtown, separated from Kick's nearly identical property by a stand of oak trees. We'd bought them five years ago, when rodeo winnings had started piling up faster than we could spend them. His property was on the left, mine on the right, and both had been designed by the same architect who'd managed to make them feel like home rather than showpieces.

Mine was a single-story modern farmhouse with clean lines and lots of glass. Stone and wood and metal combined in ways that shouldn't work, but did.

I kicked off my boots by the door, hung up my jacket, and headed straight for the kitchen. I needed another drink. Or maybe I needed to stop drinking and go to bed like Tryst had suggested.

Instead, I poured myself a glass of wine from the bottle I'd opened last night—a ten-year-old Cabernet—and carried it into the living room. I flipped the switch for the gas fireplace and dropped onto the leather sofa.

I should go to bed and try to sleep, because tomorrow was going to be a long day. Walking three different vineyard blocks, checking ripeness levels, making harvest plans. All while behaving as if my entire world hadn't shifted on its axis tonight when I kissed Saffron Hope.

I took a drink of wine and rested my head against the sofa back.

When had this happened? When had Saffron stopped being just a friend—the woman who saved me from Isabel every year at the auction—and become someone I couldn't stop thinking about?

Or had she always been this to me, and I'd never taken enough time to allow myself to think about it? Like Bit had said earlier, maybe she saw me as the guy who was never around, who spent ten months a year on the rodeo circuit, chasing buckles and prize money and glory. Why would she think I'd stick around a minute longer than I had to? Why would she accept I wanted her for more than just right now?

I closed my eyes and let myself remember the kiss. The way she'd tasted—sweet and warm and perfect. The little gasp she'd made when I deepened it, when my tongue had touched hers, still echoed in my memory. She'd pulled me closer instead of pushing me away—God, that had been heaven.

My cock hardened as I remembered the way her body had felt pressed against mine. Her soft curves against hard muscle. The way she'd risen up on her toes to get closer, to take more, drove me crazy. The little sounds she'd made in the back of her throat had driven me absolutely insane.

Instead of taking the cold shower I needed to cool myself the fuck off, I let myself imagine what would've happened if I hadn't stopped. If I hadn't demanded honesty and walked away. If I'd kept kissing her, kept touching her.

My hand dropped to my lap, and I adjusted myself through my jeans. I was rock-hard now and aching with want. My mind wandered further, imagining peeling the clothes off her body. What she was wearing should've been forgettable, but it wasn't. From the minute I'd walked into her house, I couldn't keep my eyes off how it hugged her curves.

I imagined sliding my hands under that Henley and feeling her warm skin. The thought made me groan out loud.

I'd pull that shirt over her head, kiss her neck, and feel her pulse racing under my lips. She'd tilt her head back, giving me better access. I'd take my time, learn every inch of her skin, and find every spot that made her gasp or moan or dig her nails into my shoulders.

My hand moved to my belt buckle. This was a terrible idea, and I should stop. I should go take that cold shower after all. But I didn't.

I freed myself from my jeans and wrapped my hand around my cock, hissing at the contact.

I imagined her on my bed, spread out on the dark gray sheets. She'd look up at me, equally nervous and wanting. I'd take my time undressing her and savoring every reveal. The curves of her breasts, the dip of her waist, the flare of her hips—I'd memorize every freckle, every mark, every perfect imperfection.

Then I'd put my mouth on her. I'd taste every inch of her skin and learn what made her arch her back and cry out my name. I'd take her nipple into my mouth and feel it harden against my tongue. She'd thread her fingers through my hair again, holding me there, telling me exactly what she wanted.

I'd kiss my way down her stomach and settle between her thighs. She'd be wet for me—I knew she would. I'd taste her, take my time making her come on my tongue before I ever pushed inside her.

My hand worked over my cock now, and the friction was not enough and too much all at once. I imagined the sounds she'd make when I entered her. The way she'd feel wrapped around me, hot and tight. I'd start slow and let her adjust, even though every instinct would be screaming at me to move, to take, to claim.

But I'd make it good for her. I'd make it so good she'd never want anyone else and never think about anyone but me.

I'd kiss her while I thrust hard, swallowing her every moan and gasp. She'd wrap her legs around my waist so I'd go deeper. Her nails would rake down my back, marking me and claiming me right back.

She'd say my name—not Snapper, but Salazar. The name only my family used, the name that meant something more. She'd gasp it against my mouth as she got close, as I felt her start to tighten around me.

"Salazar, please—"

I'd give her everything. I'd move faster, harder, exactly the way she needed. I'd reach between us and play with her clit, then feel her fall apart. She'd come with my name on her lips, and that would be it for me. I'd follow her over, bury myself deep, and empty everything I had into her body.

We'd collapse together, sweaty and satisfied. She'd curl into my side and trace idle lines on my chest while we both caught our breath. I'd hold her close and press a kiss to the top of her head. I'd tell her that she was mine and I was hers and nothing else mattered.

I came hard, and my body tensed as release rolled through me. I bit back the groan and rode it out, my hand still moving until the last aftershock faded. Then I slumped back against the couch, breathing hard and staring at the ceiling.

Jesus Christ. I needed to get my head on straight. Yeah, it had been a while since I'd been with a woman.

Not that any other woman would do anymore. It was Saffron or nobody. How had that thought gone from maybe to carved in stone?

I cleaned myself off with tissues from the side table and was about to head to the bedroom when my phone buzzed. I almost ignored it, thinking it would be one of my brothers checking in. Instead, when I reached for it, I saw a text from Saffron.

Thank you for wanting to help me. I'm sorry I didn't say that earlier, before you left.

I stared at the message for several seconds. She was reaching out and extending an olive branch, maybe, or just being polite. I couldn't tell.

All is forgiven, I wrote back.

Three dots appeared immediately. They disappeared, then appeared again, and I ran out of patience.

I can't stop thinking about our kiss, I wrote, hitting send before I could talk myself out of it.

This time, the dots were replaced by a message in a matter of seconds.

I can't stop thinking about it either.

My heart slammed against my ribs. *I wish I was still there.*

The dots appeared again. This time, they lasted longer, and I could picture her deleting and retyping, trying to figure out what to say and how much to admit.

Finally—*I wish you were too.*

Then, before I could reply, *Good night, Snapper.*

I set the phone down, and a stupid smile spread across my face despite everything.

She wanted me. She'd as good as admitted it. All I had to do was figure out how to get her to trust me enough that we wouldn't start this thing with secrets between us.

I headed to the bedroom, hoping I was relaxed enough now to sleep. Tomorrow, I'd see her at dawn. We'd walk the vineyards together, check the grapes, and make plans for the harvest.

And maybe, just maybe, I'd find a way to break through those walls she kept building between us.

8

Saffron

I arrived at the Zinfandel block just as the sky began lightening from deep purple-gray. The October chill bit at my exposed skin, and I hugged my jacket tighter to my body.

Headlights cut through the dim morning, and Snapper's SUV rolled to a stop at the edge of the vineyard. I watched him climb out with two travel mugs in hand.

"Morning, Saff." He held one out as he approached. "Extra cream, extra sugar. The way you like it, even though it's basically a milkshake."

I took it. "You drink yours black like a lunatic."

"I drink mine like someone with functioning taste buds." He grinned, and just like that, some of the tension eased. This was us. This was normal. Except for the part where I couldn't stop thinking about his mouth on mine last night.

"You didn't sleep," he said.

"How can you tell?"

"I've known you since before you convinced your-self you could skateboard down Dead Man's Hill. What were you? Six? Seven?"

"I made it halfway."

"You broke your wrist."

"I would've made it all the way if I hadn't." I took a sip of coffee to hide my smile. "Should we check the grapes?"

"Yeah." But he didn't move immediately. Instead, he stood there, looking at me like he was trying to fig-ure out what I was thinking. Good luck with that—I didn't even know.

We walked on opposite sides of Zinfandel vines, maintaining a buffer of space that felt both neces-sary and ridiculous. I took the refractometer out of my pocket, grateful to have something technical to focus on.

"Here." I handed it to him, then reached for a cluster.

Our fingers touched, and heat shot up my arm. We both pretended it hadn't happened, but I saw tension ripple across his shoulders.

I squeezed juice from a berry onto the device's prism while he held it up to catch the light.

"Twenty-two point three Brix," he said.

"Another couple of points, and we're there." I moved to the next vine, hyperaware of how near he was. Close enough to smell his soap and to see the shadow of stubble along his neck. Close enough to remember exactly how that stubble had felt against my skin when he'd kissed me.

I cleared my throat and focused on the grapes. "These look healthy."

"Yeah, your dad's always run a tight ship. Remember when we were kids and he caught us eating grapes straight off the vines?"

"He lectured us for twenty minutes about respecting the harvest."

"Worth it, though. Those grapes were incredible." He shot me a sideways glance. "You ate way more than I did."

"I did not."

"You had juice running down your chin."

"That's a lie, and you know it."

"Is it?" His grin was wicked. "Because I have a very clear memory of your dad making you write 'I will not steal grapes' a hundred times."

"Fifty times. And you had to do it too."

"Yeah, but I only wrote it twenty times before he gave up on me." He reached for another bunch, examining it. "He always liked you better."

That made me laugh out loud. "God, I would hope so. Although I think he always wanted a boy."

"Sons-in-law count," he said with a wink.

The easy banter felt good. Like we could do this—work together, be around each other, behave as though everything hadn't shifted between us. Until that comment. While I knew what he meant, it only reminded me of what Isabel had said about him and my sister.

We were quiet as we worked through the rest of the block, sampling from different areas. The readings stayed consistent—twenty-two to twenty-three across the board.

"Wednesday or Thursday," he said. "October fifteenth or sixteenth."

Even if the baby was born today, my parents wouldn't be back from Napa by then. It would be at least another week. Maybe two. Plenty of time for us to get what we had here picked and get the maceration started at Los Cab's facility.

"This could really happen," I said under my breath.

"Not could, *is*." He stepped closer. "You scared?"

"Terrified," I admitted.

"Of the wine? Or of me?"

"Both. Neither. I don't know." I looked away. "Can we just focus on the grapes?"

"Sure." There was an understanding in the way he said it that made me feel seen. "Ready to check our blocks?"

The drive to Los Caballeros took less than ten minutes. I'd made this trip a thousand times—for family dinners, harvest celebrations, and that time when I was sixteen and Lucia had taught me and Felicity how to make proper tamales. But today, sitting in Snapper's passenger seat with the memory of what had happened last night burning between us felt awkward.

I'd thought about taking my own vehicle, but when he insisted I ride with him, I decided it would be best not to fight him every step of the way. Now, I wished I was in my own truck, so I could freely have the conversations with myself that I so desperately needed to.

"So. We're really not going to talk about it?" he asked.

"Talk about what?"

"Saffron."

"It hasn't even been twenty-four hours. Can we have at least that long before the postmortem?" I'd meant it as a joke, but it fell flat.

"Postmortem makes it sound like something died."

"Didn't it?" I turned to look at him. "Our friendship, maybe?"

His knuckles went white on the steering wheel. "Is that what you think?"

"I don't know what I think."

"Well, I do." He glanced at me. "I think we've been dancing around this for years. I think you feel it too. And I think you're scared because if we try this and it doesn't work, you lose me."

My chest tightened. "Don't."

"Don't what? Tell the truth?"

"Don't make me talk about this when I can barely think straight."

"Come on, Saff. The texts…"

My pulse hammered, and I wished I could plug my ears.

"I meant what I said. All of it."

"I know."

"But I won't push. You need time. I can give you that."

"Thank you," I whispered.

He drove through the gates of his family's property, and I let myself breathe again, knowing that, soon, we'd be around other people, unable to talk about time or kissing or being afraid.

Cru was waiting near the Gamay block. "Morning, Saffron," he said, hugging me. "Thanks for dragging yourself out here before the sun's even all the way up."

"Are you kidding? This is the most exciting thing I've done in years." How sad was it that what I'd said as a joke was actually true?

"That's because you need to get out more." He shot Snapper a look. "Though from what I hear, you two have been spending plenty of time together lately."

"Shut up," Snapper muttered, color creeping up his neck.

I bit back a smile. The Avila brothers never missed a chance to give each other shit.

"Ma's already planning the wedding," Cru continued, widening his grin. "She's thinking spring. Maybe April."

"I will end you," Snapper seethed.

"What? I'm just saying she's been waiting for this since you were both teenagers."

"Cru—"

"Remember that time at the harvest festival when you punched Tommy Berkshire for calling Saffron fat?"

I stared. "You did what?"

"I didn't punch him," Snapper said quickly. "I shoved him. There's a difference."

"You gave him a bloody nose," Cru corrected. "Uncle Tryst grounded you for a week."

"He shouldn't have been talking about her like that."

Warmth spread throughout my body. "I didn't know about that."

"Because I handled it." Snapper's expression went hard. "Can we please check the grapes now?"

"Sure, sure." But Cru looked delighted as he led us into the vines. "Just making conversation."

We sampled the Syrah—smaller bunches than our Zinfandel, thinner skins. Cru explained the differences in the soil composition and how the limestone content affected the acidity.

"Twenty-one point eight right now," he said after checking several vines. "So we're looking at seven to ten days."

I did the mental math. "That gives us time between harvests. We won't be overwhelmed."

"Exactly. And the Gamay will come in last, probably another week after that." He glanced between us. "So, still think we can make this work?"

"Yeah," Snapper said quietly, looking at me. "Of course I do."

"Any luck finding more of Concepción's notes?" Cru asked.

"Not yet. We found her journal, but it doesn't have the formula."

"Well, you've got another two weeks before you have to resort to plan B." He glanced at his watch. "I need to get back—Daphne and I have an appointment this morning we couldn't reschedule. Snapper knows where the Syrah block is. Block twelve."

"Please tell Daph I said hello."

"Will do." He started toward his truck, then paused. "Hey, Saffron? For what it's worth, I think this is good. You two working together. It's about time."

Heat crept into my cheeks. "Thanks, Cru."

After he left, the silence felt heavier. Just Snapper and me, alone in the vineyard, with the morning sun warming the air around us.

"Cru loves busting your chops," I said.

"Yeah, he really does." But he was smiling. "Syrah's this way."

"So," I said after we'd walked for a few minutes in silence. "You punched Tommy Berkshire for me?"

"I shoved him. And he had it coming."

"What did he say?"

"Does it matter?"

"Kind of."

Snapper was quiet. "He called you the nickname your sister uses. Said some other things that weren't his business. I told him to shut up. He didn't. So I made him."

"My hero," I teased. Except, really, I meant it.

"Don't." But color flooded his face. "I was twelve and stupid."

"You were sweet."

"I was pissed off that someone was being an asshole to you."

"Still sweet." I bumped his shoulder with mine. "Even if you won't admit it."

The Syrah block came into view, tucked into a south-facing slope. The vines were full of near-perfect fruit, and I felt a surge of excitement. I reached for a bunch, rolling a berry between my fingers. "Not quite ready. Another week, maybe more."

"So October twentieth to twenty-third?" He was standing near enough that I could feel the warmth radiating off him.

"Probably." I squeezed the berry, tasting the juice. Still too acidic, the tannins sharp. "Needs more time."

I reached for another at the same moment he did, and our hands collided.

Rather than pull away, he wrapped his fingers around mine. They felt warm and strong, and my breath caught.

"Sorry," we said simultaneously.

The absurdity of it—apologizing for touching each other when last night we'd been pressed against my kitchen wall, his hands in my hair and my legs wrapped around his waist—broke something loose. I laughed, and it felt like relief.

He smiled, really smiled, and God, when had he gotten so beautiful? Or had he always been this way and I'd just been too scared to really look?

"Great minds," he said, his thumb stroking across my knuckles before he let go.

"Something like that."

After we finished sampling, we headed to the winery, and he led me into the production building.

"We'll use these for the maceration," he said, pointing to three large tanks.

I ran my hand along the cool steel, studying the monitoring systems built into the sides. The units were beautiful—clean lines, flawless welds, technology that made our equipment at Hope look ancient by comparison.

"This is ideal," I said.

"The system logs everything." He moved to a control panel, and data appeared on the screen. "Temperature, CO2 levels, pH. All of it." His fingers moved over the touchscreen, familiar and confident. "I can set it up to send alerts to both our phones. That way, we can both monitor it remotely."

Both our phones. Partners.

"Wow." I stepped closer to the screen. "Show me how it works?"

Our gazes collided, and his face was inches from mine. "Saffron?"

"Yeah?"

"You're not listening."

"I am."

"What did I just say?"

I had no idea. "Something about…temperatures?"

He half smiled. "Wrong." His sounded amused when he reached up to tuck a strand of hair behind my ear. "What are you thinking about?"

"Nothing."

"Liar."

"How do you always know when I'm lying?"

"Because I know you." His hand lingered near my face, thumb stroking along my cheekbone. "I've always known you. Let me help. That's all I'm asking," he said, cupping my cheek with his palm.

"You are helping."

He leaned closer. "You know what I mean."

I wanted to tell him everything. The foreclosure. The desperation. The fear that kept me awake at night. But I wasn't able to bring myself to.

"I, uh, need to get home. I have a lot to do before Wednesday."

Frustration flickered across his face before he smoothed it away and dropped his hand. "Let's go." I hated how angry he sounded.

The walk back through the winery felt longer than it should have. Every step echoed in the cavernous space, and the silence between us grew heavier.

We made it halfway to the parking area before Lucia appeared, waving a dish towel. "*Mija!* Perfect timing. I have breakfast ready."

I opened my mouth to decline, but she was already linking her arm through mine with the kind of determined warmth that made refusal impossible.

"You must eat. You're too skinny, and you work too hard."

I glanced at Snapper and saw the same amusement I had a few minutes ago.

"Thank you, Lucia," I said as she led us toward the house.

"I made cinnamon rolls. The good ones, not the store-bought garbage."

The kitchen smelled heavenly with coffee, cinnamon, and chorizo sizzling on the stove. Lucia settled us at the counter and started piling food on plates like we were still kids. Which, in a way, we were. She'd been feeding me since I was old enough to sit on these stools, alternating between Spanish and English as she scolded me for not eating enough vegetables or praised me for good grades or listened to me cry over mean things kids had said to me.

The memory of me complaining about Tommy Berkshire teasing me became clear as day. Why hadn't I remembered it earlier when Cru brought it up? Why hadn't Snapper reminded me?

This time when our eyes met, he reached over and squeezed my hand as if he knew what I was thinking. I expected him to let go, but he didn't.

"I was thinking about Concepción's formula for the Christmas Blessing Wine," Lucia muttered as she used a spatula to separate more of the chorizo.

"And?" Snapper prompted.

She poured coffee into handmade mugs—the same ones she'd had since I was a child, each one slightly different, made by a local potter. "There's one more place it could be."

Snapper made a gesture with his free hand for her to go on.

"In the production logs. They go back to when your fourth great-grandfather made the first wine here in California."

"What year would that have been?" I asked.

"Around 1875, if I remember right." Lucia's eyebrows flared, and she grabbed Snapper's hand from across the counter. "His name was Salazar."

"That's kinda cool," I murmured.

"No new names in this family. Everyone is named for someone."

Lucia let go and smacked the back of Snapper's hand. "We honor tradition," she said, raising her chin.

He looked sufficiently contrite for his comment that she returned to the stove.

"Where would those logs be kept?" I asked.

"In the caves, but I have no idea where," said Snapper. "The ones I've seen don't go back that far."

"They wouldn't need to. Only as far as the mid-nineteen hundreds."

"You'll look after you eat," Lucia said without glancing over at either of us. "Your grandpapa, Cristobal, would tell stories about how his mother, Concepción, could taste a wine and know everything about it. What year, which varietals were used, sometimes even who made it."

"I remember seeing something in my great-grandmother's journals about that."

Lucia looked between her son and me. "Now, there are many female winemakers. Back then, it was very rare. Concepción and Marilyn Hope received many accolades for the Christmas Blessing."

"Any idea why they decided not to make the wine again?" I asked.

She looked off in the distance for several seconds. "I remember Alfonso, Salazar's father, talking about it, but I can't remember the details. It may not have been their decision."

"Do you think their husbands wouldn't let them?" Snapper asked.

His mother rolled her eyes. "Wouldn't let them? When do you think this was, the dark ages?"

He chuckled. "It was just a theory."

Lucia muttered something under her breath I couldn't hear.

"Ma?" Snapper pressed.

"If Eduardo told Concepción she couldn't do something, he would've met with the same fate as your father if he tried it with me." She opened a drawer, took out a rolling pin, and held it up.

"Jeez, Ma, what would you have done? Smacked him with that?"

She smiled. "More than once."

While we finished breakfast, Lucia kept up her steady stream of conversation—Cru and Daphne's upcoming wedding, how Brix and Addy's daughter, Reagan, was already walking and getting into everything, questions about my parents and how Felicity was doing. "Coco told Alexis that she wanted to be a winemaker for Halloween this year," she added with a laugh.

"How old is she now?" I asked.

"Seven going on thirty, just like Alex was at that age."

Snapper lifted his fork with his left hand, since his right still held mine, and took a bite of his cinnamon roll. "What about Alfonso?"

"Like most four-year-old boys, he changes his mind every day. You were the same way. When you were his age, you wanted to be a smashing pumpkin. Your father and I had no idea what that meant until Gabriel explained it was a band. All I could envision was how much fun your brothers and sister would have covering you in pumpkin guts."

I squeezed his hand. "That's adorable."

"Don't encourage her," Snapper muttered, but he was smiling too.

"I have many stories, *mija*." Lucia's eyes sparkled with mischief. "Like the time when you two were—what, thirteen?—and you tried to make wine in the barn."

"I was eleven," I corrected. "And it was Snapper's idea."

"It was a joint idea," he muttered. "You said, and I quote, 'How hard can it be?'"

"And you said, 'Let's find out.'"

Lucia laughed. "It exploded all over the barn. Took you two days to clean up the mess, and the barn smelled like rotten fruit for weeks."

"Worth it, though," Snapper said. "We learned what not to do."

"You learned that you can't just put grape juice in jars and hope for the best," Lucia continued. "Though I suppose that's valuable too."

The warmth in this kitchen, the easy laughter, and the way Snapper's mother looked at us like we were exactly where we were supposed to be made me wistful. I loved my family, and my sister and I teased each other incessantly, but this was at a whole other level.

Not only did Snapper have six siblings, but there were ten kids in Lucia's sister's family, and they lived less than ten miles from here. Our family was so small in comparison and proportionately less fun.

When we'd finished eating and helped clean up—over Lucia's protests that I was a guest, which I ignored because I'd been helping in this kitchen since I was old enough to reach the sink—Snapper said, "I should get Saffron home. She's got prep work before Wednesday."

"Of course." Lucia hugged me. "Take care of yourself, *mija*. Don't work too hard. And don't be such a stranger. You're welcome here anytime, you know."

"I do and thank you."

She held me at arm's length, looking at me with those knowing eyes that always seemed to see too much. "You look tired. Make sure you rest, okay? You can't take care of the vineyard if you don't take care of yourself first."

"I will."

"Promise me."

"I promise."

She kissed my forehead, then turned to Snapper. "And you. Stop pestering her. Give her space to breathe."

"I'm not—"

"Yes, you are. I know my sons." She patted his cheek. "Be patient."

He flushed. "Yes, ma'am."

The drive back to my family's place was quiet at first. Snapper kept his eyes on the road, but his jaw was tight. I stared out the window, watching vineyards roll past, thinking about everything and nothing.

"My mom's right," he said. "I am pestering you."

"You're not."

"I am. I keep pushing when I said I wouldn't."

"Snapper—"

"No, let me finish." He took a breath. "I meant what I said about giving you time. About not going anywhere. But I also meant what I said in that text. I want you to know I'm choosing this. Choosing you. Before anything else comes up that makes you doubt it."

"Why?"

"Why what?"

"Why me? Why now? You've had your pick of women for years. Buckle bunnies, Isabel throwing herself at you every chance she gets, probably a dozen others I don't even know about."

"You really don't know?"

"No."

"Because it's always been you, Saffron." He glanced at me, then back at the road. "Since we were kids. Since before I even knew what it meant to want someone. You've always been the one I looked for in a room. The one I wanted to tell things to. The one who made me want to be better."

"Snapper—"

"I know the timing is shit. I know you're dealing with something you won't tell me about. And getting involved with me is probably the last thing you need right now. But I'm tired of acting like we're just friends when we both know it's more than that."

"What if it doesn't work? What if we try this and—"

"Then we'll deal with it. But at least we'll know."

"Your friendship means a lot to me. I don't want to lose that."

"You won't." His voice was firm. "That's what I'm trying to tell you. Even if the romantic stuff doesn't work—and I think it will, but even if it doesn't—you're not losing me. I know I keep repeating it, but I'm not going anywhere."

I wanted to believe him so badly it hurt.

He drove up to my house and put the truck in park, but neither of us moved.

"Thanks for this morning," I said.

"We're partners."

"Yes, and I'll text you tomorrow with an update on the readings."

He faced me, and the intensity in his gaze made me pause.

"I need to go. Lots to prep." I pushed the door open before I could do something stupid like climb across the console and kiss him again.

He let me go. Again. Patient in a way I didn't deserve, giving me the space I'd asked for even though I could see how much it cost him.

I headed toward the house, forcing myself not to look back. If I did, I wouldn't keep walking.

I made it to the porch before I heard his truck start. The sound of it driving away tugged at something in my chest, like a tether stretching too far.

Inside, the house was too empty, too quiet.

My phone buzzed almost immediately. *Saffron...* then dots appeared, but no message followed.

Just my name. But it felt like everything—a question, a promise, and a plea.

I'm sorry, I wrote, unsure what exactly I was apologizing for.

When the dots appeared again, disappeared, then reappeared, I held my breath.

What I wanted to say but couldn't is, I want you so much that when we're together, it's hard to breathe.

It was exactly how I felt but wasn't brave enough to say.

Would he give me the space I needed, or would he run out of patience?

See you tomorrow. If I can wait that long. He added a winking emoji.

God, I hoped he couldn't.

9

Snapper

I'd barely slept. Every time I closed my eyes, I felt her pressed against me in the kitchen, tasted wine on her lips, and heard that small sound she'd made when I kissed her neck. That had been two nights ago, but my body didn't seem to care. It wanted her like it had just happened. I checked my phone before my eyes were fully open. There were no new messages from Saffron, no response to me saying I'd see her today, if I could wait that long. Had I really thought there would be? Wished, yes. Expected, no way.

Instead of putting the phone down like I should have, I opened my photos. I had so many of her—of us—spanning years. Harvest celebrations where she stood laughing with grape juice staining her hands. The summer she was seventeen and worked alongside Kick and me, her ponytail pulled through a Los Cab baseball cap. The previous Wicked Winemakers' Ball, where she wore the same dress she had this year, her smile genuine before Isabel cornered her. A candid shot from three years ago, when she didn't know I was watching, standing in the vineyard at sunset with her eyes closed and face turned toward the sun like she was soaking in the last warmth of the day.

I hadn't been able to bring myself to delete a single one, even when I told myself I was being pathetic.

I closed the photo app and sent her a message. *Going to look for those logs Ma mentioned. Want to help?*

The dots appeared right away, disappeared, then started again.

What time?

An hour? Meet you at the caves?

I'll be there.

I stared at the screen for another few seconds, then forced myself to move. Shower, clothes, fresh coffee. Every minute dragged while I waited.

The drive to Los Cab took forever despite being less than twenty minutes from my house in town. When I arrived at the caves, Saffron's truck was already there. She stood near the driver's side door with her arms crossed and her hair in a ponytail that made her look ten years younger.

"You're early," I said, climbing out.

"So are you."

We stood there for several seconds, neither of us moving.

"Ready?" I asked.

"Lead the way."

I took her past the main barrel room, where hundreds of French oak barrels sat, aging wine in neat rows, their surfaces already developing the purple-black stains that came from years of use. The air smelled like wood and wine and time—earthy and rich.

We took the left fork into the east branch. Back here, the passages narrowed and the ceiling dropped lower.

"I've never been this far into the caves," Saffron said.

"Not many people have."

The storage area opened up ahead—still carved from the same hillside stone but fitted with modern shelving units that held boxes and crates stacked from floor to ceiling. A single wooden table sat in the center with two chairs that looked like they'd been there since my grandfather's time.

"Where do we start?" Saffron moved to the nearest shelf, running her finger along the edge of a dusty box.

"Ma said Tryst organized everything about ten years ago. So there's some kind of system."

"Theoretically."

I reached for the first box and set it on the table. Inside, we found production logs from the 1980s—my father's handwriting, strong and angular, recording tonnage and Brix levels and fermentation temperatures. I flipped through a few pages, then set it aside.

Saffron opened the next box. "Nineteen seventies." She looked at me. "We're going backward in time."

"Then we keep going."

We fell into a rhythm. Pull a box, check the dates, set it aside if it was from the wrong decade. The next shelf back held logs from the sixties. Then the fifties. Each decade took us deeper into the past, into handwriting that grew more ornate, ink that faded to sepia, and paper that felt thin enough to crumble.

"Look at this!" She opened a leather-bound book that was cracked with age. "December 1955."

I moved to look over her shoulder. Tucked between two pages near the back, there was a folded piece of paper. She gasped as we both read what was on the page.

Christmas Blessing Wine Blend
Gamay: 40%
Syrah: 35%
Zinfandel: 25%

Beneath the varietals and percentages, there were detailed notes about temperatures, timing, CO2 levels for the carbonic maceration, how long to let it ferment, and when to rack it. Everything we needed.

"Oh my God." Saffrons said barely above a whisper. "This is it. This is actually it." She turned in my arms—when had I put them around her?—and looked up at me with eyes that were bright with unshed tears. "We found it."

Then she was hugging me, her face pressed against my chest, her arms tight around my waist.

I held her, one hand sliding into her hair and the other splayed across her back. I wanted to sink into her and allow myself to feel the same relief and happiness she felt, except I couldn't. Not until she admitted why making the wine this year was so important.

Tell me, I silently screamed. *Trust me.*

She leaned away just enough to look at me. Couldn't she feel my hurt even if she didn't see it?

"Let me take you to dinner tonight," I said after several seconds of silence. "To celebrate."

Her brow furrowed. "You don't have to—"

"I want to. A real dinner. Not my mom's kitchen or the diner. Somewhere special."

"Snapper—"

"Please, Saff. Let me do this."

She hesitated before answering. "Okay. What time?"

"I'll pick you up at seven."

"Okay," she repeated, softer this time.

After Saffron got in her truck and left, I called Bit.

"Where are you?" I asked.

"Here. At the Stonehouse."

"Be there in a minute."

He and Eberly were waiting near the entrance when I arrived at the original winery building that sat at the heart of Los Caballeros.

"We found the formula for the Christmas wine," I blurted as I got out of my truck.

His eyebrows shot up. "That's—wow. Congratulations."

"Thanks, and now, I need your help."

"You got it. What can I do?"

"It's about Saffron."

Slow grins spread across both his face and Eberly's as they motioned for me to follow them.

"Oh no," Eberly said once we were inside. "He's got that look."

"What look?" I asked.

"The one that means we're about to help you do something ill-advised," Bit responded.

"It's not ill-advised. I just—" I ran a hand through my hair. "I want to take her to dinner tonight. To celebrate finding the formula. But not just any dinner. Something…I don't know. Special. Private. Romantic. All of that."

Bit gestured around us. "What about here?"

I looked at the space like I was seeing it for the first time. The original fermentation room stretched before us—massive stone walls, with its exposed wood beams crossing the vaulted ceiling. Lights were strung above the tables, where candles and floral arrangements already sat.

I could see the garden courtyard through the floor-to-ceiling windows and could imagine Saffron along the pathways that wound through wild roses, ivy, and lavender.

"Can I?" I asked.

"It's not booked tonight," Bit said, looking at Eberly. "What do you think?"

She smiled. "It's perfect. Give me until five o'clock, and I'll have everything ready."

"You don't have to—"

"I know I don't have to. I want to." She squeezed my arm. "You said you wanted special, private, and romantic. There isn't anywhere on the Central Coast that fits the bill better than this does. Now, I need to put the menu together." She looked at Bit. "Then you can do the wine pairings."

After she left, Bit gestured for me to sit at the bar. I rested my arms on its top as exhaustion settled over me.

"So, you're really doing this," he said.

"Making the wine? Yep. Sure are."

"That's not what I meant. You're going all in with Saffron?"

I thought about arguing, but what was the point? "Yeah. I am."

"Good." He took a sip from the coffee cup I hadn't noticed he brought with him. "She's worth it."

"I know she is. I just—" I stopped, trying to figure out how to explain how I felt. "What if I screw this up?"

"You won't."

"I appreciate the vote of confidence."

"Look, I know you." He nudged me. "You're one of the most stubborn, determined people I've ever met.

When you want something, you don't give up. And you want her."

"I do."

"Then stop overthinking it, and just be yourself. That's who she wants anyway. One more thing," Bit said. "Whatever happens tonight, whatever she does or doesn't tell you—don't push."

"I know."

"Do you? Because you've got that look like you're about to storm a castle."

"I'm not storming anything. I'm just tired of knowing she's drowning and won't let me throw her a rope, because she doesn't trust that I can see her going under."

Bit's expression softened. "She'll tell you. When she's ready."

"You said I'm going all in with her, but I can't, Bit. Not until she tells me what I already know. I want her. I have for years, but she still refuses to admit the reason making the wine now is so important is because, if she doesn't, her family will lose everything."

"I'd tell you to be patient, but if I were in your shoes, I wouldn't be able to be."

"Thanks for admitting it."

"Of course. Now, I better get in there and help my wife before she has a menu better suited for twenty rather than two."

"You're sure this is okay?"

Bit cocked his head. "This place is as much yours as it is mine. You don't need my permission to have dinner here."

"But I do need you and Eberly to make it."

"Yeah, we've got you."

10

Saffron

The drive home from Los Caballeros should have felt triumphant. We'd found it—Concepción's half of the formula, complete with percentages and techniques and everything we needed to actually make the Christmas Blessing Wine. Instead, guilt sat in my passenger seat like an unwelcome hitchhiker.

I'd stood in the cave, with Snapper's arms around me, his chest pressed against my back, both of us staring at what his great-grandmother had written, knowing it could literally save my family, and I still hadn't told him why it mattered so much. Why it had to be this Christmas. Why I was so desperate I could barely breathe sometimes.

I parked in the driveway and sat in my truck for several minutes, staring at the house. It looked the same as always. Like I was seeing it through glass, something beautiful but untouchable, already slipping away.

Silence hit me when I walked inside. No Mom humming in the kitchen. Dad's boots weren't by the door.

No sounds of anyone moving around upstairs. Just me and the quiet and too many thoughts I didn't want to think.

I dropped my purse on the counter and stood in the kitchen, trying to figure out what to do with myself. Snapper wouldn't pick me up for dinner until seven. That gave me—I checked my phone—almost eight hours to fill.

Eight hours alone with my thoughts sounded like torture.

I changed into work clothes and went outside. The October afternoon was warm, the kind of perfect fall day that reminded me why I loved wine country. I walked through our Zin block, running my hands over leaves that had started their autumn shift from green to gold and rust. The clusters appeared almost ready.

Wednesday or Thursday. That's when we'd harvest. Two days, maybe three.

This was really happening. We were really going to make this wine, but what if it didn't work? What if it wasn't any good? What if the wine that everyone said was "legendary" was just average? More of an urban myth?

"You better be worth it." I muttered to myself. "You better produce the best damn juice there's ever been."

The stalks didn't answer, but I hadn't expected them to. I'd been talking to these plants since I was old enough to walk their rows with my father. He used to say that vines could sense intention, that they knew when they were loved and tended with care versus when they were just a crop to be harvested and sold.

I hoped he was right. I hoped these grapes understood what was riding on them.

I spent an hour checking the fruit for any signs of disease or stress. Everything looked good. Healthy. Ready. Then I headed to the winery building to look over our equipment—the bins we'd need for handpicking, the small sorting table we rarely used anymore, the bins that would carry what we picked to Los Caballeros for processing.

My phone rang just as I was coming back outside. Felicity's name lit up the screen.

"Hey, how are you feeling?" I asked.

"Still pregnant. Still huge. But good."

"Any signs of labor?"

"Not yet. The doctor says it could still be another few days." She paused. "Bored now that the harvest is over?"

Bored? "I have plenty of work to keep up with until Dad gets back."

"I swear, one of these years, you should make Snapper actually take you on a date." Felicity's tone softened. "You've basically been running things for years, Saff. Dad could probably retire."

Had I? It didn't feel that way. It felt like I'd been scrambling to keep up, patching holes, making do with equipment that should have been replaced a decade ago, stretching every dollar until it screamed. I just hadn't realized why until last week.

"So listen," Felicity continued. "I was just thinking about how crazy it is. Wagner and the baby and our winery and this whole life we've built—I never dreamed I could be this happy, you know? Like, I didn't even know this was possible."

"That's great, sis. I'm really happy for you."

"Thanks, pumpkin." She paused. "Are you okay? You sound weird."

"I'm fine. Just tired."

"You work too hard."

Rich, coming from my sister who'd helped her husband with their harvest while eight months pregnant. But I didn't say that.

Instead, I asked a question I knew I shouldn't. "Is Wagner the only man you've ever loved?"

The question hung in the air for several seconds. I almost took it back, almost laughed it off as a joke, but something kept me quiet.

"That's random," she muttered.

"I know. Sorry. I just—I was thinking about how you two are so perfect together, and I wondered if you'd ever—" I stopped, unsure how to finish.

"If I'd ever what?"

"If there was anyone else. Before him."

Another pause, longer this time. "I thought I loved someone once," she said quietly. "But I really didn't. It was lust or infatuation or something that wasn't love. Not like this. Not like what I have with Wagner." She laughed, but it sounded forced. "Why are we talking about this?"

"No reason. Just curious."

"Well, stop being curious about my past and start being curious about your future. Speaking of which, any interesting men in your life I should know about?"

Snapper's face flashed through my mind. His hands on my waist in the kitchen. His mouth on mine. The way he'd looked at me in the caves this morning like I was precious.

"Since Saturday? Fat chance."

"Liar. I can hear it in your voice. But fine, keep your secrets." She yawned. "I should go. Mom says I should sleep as much as I can now since once the baby is here, I won't be able to. Which reminds me, you're still coming right? I need my sister."

"You know it. I love you, Felicity."

"Love you too, pumpkin."

After she hung up, I stood in the driveway, staring at my phone.

I thought I loved someone once, but I really didn't.

What Isabel said the other night came rushing back. *You didn't know about Felicity and Snapper?*

No. I wouldn't do this. I wouldn't let Isabel's poison twist everything into something ugly.

But the doubt remained, a small seed taking root.

I was still standing in the same spot when a car drove through the front gate. A sedan I didn't recognize at first, then did—Isaac Brennan's Lexus. He worked at

First Coastal Bank. We'd gone to high school together, though he was three years ahead of me.

My heart pounded as he climbed out of the car.

"Saffron." He smiled, but it didn't reach his eyes. "Is your father home?"

"No. He's in Napa with my mom and sister. Felicity's about to have a baby."

"Oh, that's right. I forgot. Congratulations." He shifted his weight, clearly uncomfortable. "When will he be back?"

"I'm not sure. Why?"

"I just needed to speak with him about—" He stopped. "It's bank business. Nothing urgent."

Liar. Everything about his body language screamed urgent.

My courage built slowly, like water rising. "I know about the foreclosure, Isaac. How bad is it? Really?"

His expression shifted to pity. "Saffron—"

"Please. Just tell me."

"You should talk to your father."

"That's not an answer."

"It's the only one I can give you." He looked away, toward the vineyard, then back at me. "I'm sorry."

We stood in awkward silence as a hawk circled overhead, riding the thermal currents.

"Saffron," he began. "You know you don't have to carry the world on your shoulders, right? This isn't your doing or your responsibility."

I couldn't speak.

"Your father has been in this business for years, and his father before him, just like most of us in the valley," he continued. "Some of the decisions he made worked out; others didn't. But none of that is on you."

"It feels like it is."

"I know. But it's not." He squeezed my shoulder once, then retreated to his car. "Tell your dad to call me when he gets back, okay?"

I nodded and waved as he drove away.

I stood still until the dust settled. Until I could breathe again without feeling like my chest was caving in.

You don't have to carry the world on your shoulders.

Didn't I? Who would if not me?

When had that happened? When had I decided that my life didn't matter as much as everyone else's?

Isaac's words and Felicity's conversation swirled together in my head as I went inside. My sister had chosen herself and found happiness—a husband who adored her, a baby on the way, a winery of her own. She'd left and thrived.

What would happen if I chose myself?

The thought was so foreign it almost made me laugh. Choose myself how? I was already doing what I wanted—making this wine, saving the winery. Except was that really what I wanted? Or was it just another version of making myself useful and sacrificing what I needed so everyone else could be okay?

I looked at my phone. It was three-thirty, and Snapper would be here in less than four hours to take me to dinner. *Dinner.* A real date. Not breakfast at the diner. Something special, he'd said.

I climbed the stairs to my bedroom and stood in front of my closet. Most of what hung in it was practical—jeans and work shirts and jackets that had seen better days. A few dresses for weddings and funerals and the occasional charity event. Nothing special.

Then I saw it, pushed to the back—the green velvet dress. Felicity had given it to me three years ago for my birthday. "You need something beautiful," she'd said. "Something that makes you feel like the gorgeous woman you are instead of the workhorse you've become."

I'd never worn it. It felt too fancy, too impractical. When would I even wear something like this?

Tonight, apparently.

I took it out of the closet and laid it on my bed, then started the shower. I took my time—shaved my legs, deep-conditioned my hair, and used the expensive body wash I'd been saving for some undefined special occasion. When I got out, I actually blow-dried my hair instead of letting it air-dry into its usual waves.

The dress fit perfectly, hugging my waist before flowing to just above my knees. I put on makeup—not much, but enough. Mascara, a touch of blush, and lip gloss that made my mouth look fuller.

I stood in front of my mirror, barely recognizing the woman looking back.

When had I stopped doing this? When had I decided that being invisible was safer than being seen? Somewhere along the way, I'd convinced myself that wanting to look pretty was frivolous. That spending time on myself was selfish. That I didn't deserve nice things or special attention or someone like Snapper looking at me the way he did.

But tonight—tonight, I was choosing to be visible. Choosing to want something just for me. Not because it served a purpose or helped someone else or kept everything from falling apart.

The realization was equally terrifying and exhilarating.

Once downstairs, I poured myself a glass of wine, then changed my mind and dumped it down the sink. I needed to be clearheaded tonight. Enough to tell Snapper the truth about the foreclosure, about why this wine had to be made and had to be made now.

Except what if telling him changed everything? What if he looked at me with pity instead of desire? What if he realized I was just desperate and convenient and not worth all the trouble?

No. I couldn't think like that. Snapper had said I mattered to him. Had laid everything out there in my kitchen three nights ago when he'd kissed me. He'd even texted, saying he wanted me so much it was hard to breathe.

He meant it. I had to believe he meant it.

But a new fear crept in, one I hadn't let myself fully examine before.

What if the wine worked? What if it saved us and I got Snapper, and everything I'd been working toward actually happened?

What then?

I'd spent so long defining myself by struggle and sacrifice. By holding everything together through sheer force of will. If I didn't have to do that anymore—if the winery was safe and my family was okay and I had Snapper and an actual future that included things I wanted instead of just things I needed—who would I be?

The thought was almost more terrifying than losing everything.

Because I knew how to survive loss. I knew how to keep going when things were hard. But I had no idea how to handle being happy without feeling guilty about it.

Headlights swept across the kitchen window.

I checked my phone. Six forty-five. He was early.

I grabbed my wrap from the hook by the door and took one last look in the hall mirror. The woman looking back was beautiful and terrified and hopeful all at once.

I took a deep breath.

Tonight, I'd tell him about everything. I'd trust him the way he'd been asking me to.

He knocked, and a second later, I opened the door.

"Hi," I said, suddenly feeling self-conscious. Like I was overdressed.

His eyes widened, and his mouth hung open. "You look so beautiful, sweetheart."

Heat flooded my cheeks as I looked at the dark cords that sat low on his hips, the button-down shirt that stretched across his shoulders, and his hair still damp like he'd just gotten out of the shower.

"Thank you. You clean up pretty nice yourself."

His gaze traveled from my face down my body and back up again in a way that made my skin prickle with awareness. "Ready?"

"Ready." I locked the door behind me and let him lead me to his truck, his hand on the small of my back burning through the velvet of my dress.

Whatever happened tonight—whatever I told him, however he reacted—at least I'd know I'd tried. At least I'd chosen to be brave instead of safe. I just prayed I could go through with it.

11

Snapper

I spent the afternoon trying to keep busy and failing miserably. I reviewed the harvest plan even though I knew it could change multiple times before we were certain it was time to pick. After pacing around my house like a caged animal for too long, I gave up and went for a run.

At four-thirty, I showered and stood in front of my closet, trying to figure out what the hell to wear. Jeans felt too casual. Dress pants felt too formal. I settled on dark cords and a button-down shirt, then immediately second-guessed myself and was about to change when my phone buzzed with a text from Eberly. *Everything's ready. You're going to love it.*

At six-thirty, I gave up on waiting and headed to Saffron's house even though I could make the drive in an easy ten minutes. Still, it felt like an hour. When I arrived at her house, my palms were sweating.

Get it together, Avila.

I made it up the porch steps and knocked before I could talk myself into getting in my truck and coming back in fifteen minutes—when I was actually supposed to arrive. When the door opened, every coherent thought I'd ever had evaporated.

Saffron wore a deep-green dress that looked like it was made of velvet. It was fitted at the waist, then flowed from there to hit just above her knees. Her hair was down, falling in soft waves past her shoulders, and she'd put on makeup—not much, but enough that her eyes looked bigger and her lips so soft that it made me want to kiss her.

"Ready?" I asked after telling her how beautiful she looked.

"Where are we going?"

"You'll see," I said, leading her outside.

I opened the passenger door and tried not to stare at her legs as she climbed in. Tried and failed.

The air on the return trip to Los Cab felt like it did before a thunderstorm. Saffron kept her hands folded in her lap, occasionally glancing over at me like she wanted to say something but couldn't bring herself to. Or maybe that was just wishful thinking on my part.

"You're being very mysterious about this," she commented.

"Is that a bad thing?"

She smiled. "I don't know yet."

I drove through the main gates and took the west road that led to the Stonehouse. I parked near the entrance and came around to open Saffron's door.

"I haven't been here since Bit and Eberly transformed it into this," she said, waving her hands at the garden. "Snapper, it's..." she started as I led her inside.

"Do you like it?"

"Like it? I—" She stepped forward slowly, taking it all in—the wine already breathing on the table, the food being kept warm in covered dishes.

She shook her head. "No one's ever done anything like this for me before."

"No?" I helped her with her chair, and she sat, still looking around as though she couldn't believe it was real. I poured the first wine—a Pinot Noir from three years ago that I knew was one of our best—and settled across from her.

"To finding the formula," I said, raising my glass.

She touched hers to mine. "To finding the formula."

We drank, and I watched her close her eyes as the wine hit her tongue. She'd always done that, ever since we were teenagers sneaking tastes during harvest. Like she needed to shut out the world to really focus on what she was drinking.

"This is incredible," she said.

"Wait until you try the food."

Eberly had outdone herself. There was duck confit with roasted root vegetables, a salad with figs and goat cheese tossed in a citrusy dressing, and fresh bread that was still warm. All of it was perfect, so much better than if I'd taken her to a restaurant in town.

We ate in silence for a few minutes. Saffron spoke first.

"Can I ask you something?"

"Anything."

"Your shoulder." She gestured at it. "How bad is it? And don't give me the line about how it's getting better. I want the truth."

I set my fork down and flexed my arm instinctively. "Bad enough that I can't compete this year. Maybe not next year either."

"That must be killing you. Rodeo is—"

"Was," I corrected. "Rodeo *was* my life."

Her brow rose. "Was?"

"I was thinking about retiring long before I was injured."

"Did Kick know?"

I shook my head. "That was the hard part. We're a team. I'm the header, he's the heeler. You don't just go out and find a roping partner. It takes years to get as in sync as we are."

"Won't you miss it?"

"I've thought about it long enough to know I won't."

"I never thought I'd hear you say that."

I chuckled. "Me either, but like with any professional sport, you age out quick."

"Men older than you compete."

I nodded once. "Men older than me might not have as good a reason to stay home as I do."

Her doubtful expression ate at me, but the only way I knew to convince her I meant it, was by doing it.

She took another sip of wine, her gaze never leaving my face. "What will you do instead?"

"Stay here. Work the winery. Actually learn the business side instead of just showing up for harvest and then disappearing again." I paused, then rested my elbows on the table. "Build something that lasts."

"With your brothers."

"Not just them…" I stopped myself before I could finish that thought. *Maybe with you.*

It was too much, too soon.

But she was watching me like she could read my mind anyway. "Who else?"

"You already know who, Saff. But I'm not sure you're ready to hear me actually say it."

"What if I am?"

I rested against my chair, wishing she truly was. Until she could bring herself to confide in me, I'd gone as far with this conversation as I was willing to go.

"What about you?" I asked instead of telling her what she wanted to hear. "What do you want?"

Her laugh was hollow. "Besides making this wine?"

The opening was right there. I held my breath, waiting for her to say it. To tell me about the foreclosure, to admit why recreating this wine mattered so much.

"Yeah. Besides that. If you could do anything, be anything, have anything—what would it be?"

She stared at her wineglass, tracing the rim with one finger. "I don't know."

"Come on. There has to be something."

"I don't—" She stopped, then started again. "I've never let myself think about it. Everything's always been about the winery. About keeping things going. About not letting my family down."

I reached across the table and took her hand. She startled at the contact but didn't pull away. "Think about it now. If you had no obligations at all—what would Saffron Hope want?"

She was quiet for so long I thought she might not say anything, but she eventually did. "I'd want to travel. See the places where wine comes from instead of just reading about them in books. Walk through vineyards in Burgundy and Tuscany and Rioja. Taste wines that have been made the same way for centuries."

"That's a good start."

"I'd want to learn more. Languages. Art. History. All the things I didn't have time for because I was too busy in the vineyard."

"Keep going."

"I'd want—" She stopped, looking down at our joined hands. "I've never been out of the United States. How sad is that? I read about Paris and Rome and Barcelona, but I've never actually gone anywhere. I watch cooking shows about Italian food and French pastries, but I make the same ten meals on rotation because that's what I know how to make. I have travel books loaded into my e-reader that I've read from start to finish, but the farthest I've ever been from home is New York for a wine conference three years ago."

The way she spoke sounded more like she was admitting to crimes instead of just being human.

"Why not?" I asked gently.

"Because there's always been a reason not to. Dad needed help with the harvest. Mom needed help with the tasting room. Felicity got married and moved away, so someone had to stay. The vines didn't perform more than one year in a row. Every harvest, more equipment breaks down. There was always something more important than…"

"Than what?"

She shook her head and her eyes filled with tears. "I'm twenty-eight years old, and I've made myself so small that I don't even know how to want things anymore." She eased her hand away and wrapped her arms around herself. "I stopped dreaming about anything beyond next week's work schedule. I stopped thinking about my life as something that could be different."

Her vulnerability made my chest ache. "Saff—"

"You asked what I wanted, and that's the truth. I want to remember what it feels like to want something just because I want it, not because it serves some purpose or helps someone else or keeps everything from falling apart. I want to be selfish for once in my life and not feel guilty about it."

I stood and moved around the table, pulling her to her feet. "Then be selfish. Right now. Tell me one thing you want that has nothing to do with anyone else."

She looked up at me, her eyes wide and vulnerable. "I want to stop being terrified every second of every day."

"Terrified of what?"

"Of this." She gestured between us. "Of wanting you this much. Of letting myself feel something real instead of just safe."

I framed her face with my palms. "I know you don't think you can trust me, but I'll keep saying you can, proving you can until you're ready to."

"What if you get tired of waiting?"

"I won't."

"How can you be so sure?"

"Because I've been waiting for you my whole life."

She stared at me for several seconds, then rose up on her toes and kissed me. It was soft and tentative, like she was testing whether I might disappear if she pushed too hard.

I kissed her back, keeping it gentle even though every instinct screamed at me to deepen it, to take more, to show her exactly how much I meant what I'd said. But Bit's warning replayed in my head. *Let her set the pace.*

She broke the kiss. "I'm sorry I'm such a mess."

"You're not a mess."

"I am. I'm scared and confused, and I don't know what I'm doing with any of this."

"None of that makes you a mess. It makes you human." I tucked a strand of hair behind her ear. "And for what it's worth, I don't know what I'm doing either. I'm figuring it out as I go too."

"You seem pretty sure of yourself."

"Only because I'm sure about you."

She laughed, watery and rough. "That makes one of us."

"Finish eating," I said, guiding her back to her chair. "Then dance with me."

"What?"

"Dance with me. We found the formula today. We're starting the harvest tomorrow or the next day. We're going to make this wine, and it's going to be incredible. So tonight, just for a little while, let yourself celebrate that."

She looked at me like I'd suggested we fly to the moon. "I don't think I remember how to celebrate."

"Then, I'll remind you."

Our conversation shifted to lighter topics as we finished our meal. She asked about my brothers, about the rodeo circuit, about stupid things Kick and I had done as kids. I asked how her parents were, and we laughed when she reminded me about the time she tried to convince her dad to let her get a horse and ended up with a barn cat instead.

By the time we'd eaten every bite of food and drained the bottle of Pinot, some of the tension had eased from her shoulders.

I stood and held out my hand. "Come here."

She let me help her to her feet, and I led her to the open space between the table and the doors. No music played, just the sound of crickets and the rustle of wind outside the solid rock walls of the room. I gathered her close to me, one hand at her waist and the other clasping hers against my chest.

"I'm a terrible dancer," she murmured.

"Good thing I'm not."

"I hate to think how you got so good at it."

"My ma. She taught every single one of us, even Alex. I grew up two-steppin' in our kitchen."

I swayed, slow and easy, keeping her near enough that I could feel every inhale and exhale. She rested her head against my chest, and I pressed my cheek to the top of her hair.

She hadn't asked, but this was exactly what I wanted. Saffron Hope in my arms, every day for the rest of my life. It felt so right. Like this was where I was supposed to be. That she completed me. If only she'd let me all the way in.

We moved in small circles, neither of us talking, both of us wrapped in this moment that felt stolen from time. Her body fit against mine like it had been designed for it. Her hand gripped my good shoulder, and her fingers curled into the fabric of my shirt. Mine splayed across her lower back, holding her steady.

After a while, she lifted her head and looked up at me. Her eyes were darker in the candlelight, and I could feel her pulse quicken where my thumb rested against her wrist.

"Snapper," she whispered.

I kissed her. Not like the desperate, consuming kiss in her kitchen. This one was slower, deeper, a question instead of a demand. I stopped moving and cupped her face with both hands, tasting the wine on her lips, hearing her whimpers of desire.

Her hands slid up my chest, around my neck, and into my hair. She opened her mouth under mine, and I was lost. Everything narrowed to the sensation of her—soft curves pressing against hard muscle, fingers pulling my hair, and the little gasps she made when I changed the angle of the kiss.

I walked her backward until she was pressed against the wall of the Stonehouse, never breaking contact. My hands moved from her face to her waist, pulling her tighter against me. She arched into me, her leg hooking around my calf, and I groaned.

She kissed me again, harder this time, and I stopped thinking. Stopped trying to be patient. Stopped pretending this wasn't exactly what I'd wanted since I was old enough to know what wanting meant.

When I gripped her hips and she moaned, the sound snapped something inside me. I lifted her, and she wrapped her legs around my waist. I kissed her neck, her jaw, her mouth again.

"We should—" She gasped. "We should stop."

"Why?"

"Because—" She broke off when I found the spot just below her ear that made her shiver. "Because I can't think when you do that."

"Good."

"Snapper." This time, it came out as a plea.

I leaned away enough to look at her. Her pupils were blown wide, her lips swollen, her chest heaving. She looked absolutely wrecked, and it was the most beautiful thing I'd ever seen.

"Tell me to stop," I said. "If you want me to stop, just say it."

Rather than respond, she unwrapped her legs from around my waist and slid her feet to the floor.

"I'm sorry," she said, not meeting my eyes. "I just—I can't—"

"You don't have to explain."

"I want to. But—"

"But you're not ready." I ran a hand through my hair, my every nerve ending on fire, every muscle coiled tight with want. But without words, she'd asked me to stop, so I stopped. "It's okay, Saff."

"It's not okay. I just—" She eased around me, returned to the table, and sat down.

"Hey." I sat beside her. "You get to decide what you're ready for. Always. I'm not going to push you."

"Even though I'm driving you crazy?"

"Especially because you're driving me crazy." I tried to smile. "It means you feel something too."

She looked up at me then, and the vulnerability in her expression nearly broke me. "I do feel something. That's what scares me."

"I know."

"Do you? Because I don't think you understand how terrifying this is for me. Wanting someone as much as I do you. Needing you this much. It feels like standing on the edge of a cliff with my eyes closed."

I wanted to tell her I'd catch her if she fell—that I already knew about the foreclosure and would do any-thing to help her. But I couldn't. Not without admitting I'd been keeping secrets too. Not without forcing her hand when she needed to come to me on her own.

"We should go," she said, the moment fracturing. "It's getting late."

I wanted to argue, demand she stay so we could talk this through, but I didn't.

I heard Bit again in my head. *Don't push. Let her set the pace.*

So I just said, "Okay."

The drive back to her house was thick with tension. Both of us were wound too tight, both of us wanted things we couldn't have. At least not yet.

I parked in her driveway and walked her to the door, with my hands shoved in my pockets.

"Thank you for tonight," she said.

"We start harvest tomorrow. Zinfandel."

"What time?" she asked, her gaze not meeting mine.

"Dawn. I'll text you."

"Snapper?"

"Yeah?"

She rose up on her toes and kissed me. Brief, soft, over before I could really register it. "Thank you," she said again. "For all of it."

I stood on her porch after she disappeared inside, willing my pulse to slow and my body to accept that we weren't getting what we wanted tonight. After several seconds, I got in my truck and drove home.

My house felt empty and too quiet when I walked in. I stripped off my shirt, poured myself a glass of water I didn't drink, and stared at my phone, willing it to ring. Instead, it vibrated with a text.

Tonight was...

The dots appeared and disappeared three times before *thank you* appeared. *It was wonderful. Like a dream.*

I'll make all your dreams come true, if you'll let me.

Her response came faster this time—*Maybe I will.*

I set the phone down and dropped onto the couch, staring at the ceiling. My body still hummed with want, every nerve ending alive with the memory of her pressed against me. But underneath the frustration was something else. Hope.

She'd opened up tonight. Told me things she'd never said before. Admitted she'd made herself small, that she'd stopped dreaming, that she'd never even left the States.

Those weren't the words of someone who didn't trust me. They were the words of someone learning how.

Tomorrow, we'd start the harvest. Tomorrow, we'd begin the real work of making this wine. Tomorrow, we'd take the formula we'd found and turn it into something that might just give her the freedom to do what she wanted rather than what everyone else needed.

12

Saffron

I'd been in the vineyard since four in the morning, walking the rows with my flashlight and refractometer even though I'd checked the Brix levels yesterday. And the day before. The numbers hadn't changed. Twenty-four point two. Perfect for harvest.

I just needed to see them one more time.

Headlights cut across the vineyard as the sky started to lighten. Snapper's truck.

He climbed out, carrying two travel mugs, and crossed to where I stood among the vines.

"You're early," I said.

"So are you." He held out one of the mugs.

I took it and sipped.

"The crew will be here in twenty minutes." I turned back to the vines, studying the clusters I'd already examined a dozen times. "I want to start in the north section. The fruit there gets the most sun exposure, so it should be—"

"Saff."

"What?"

"Look at me."

I didn't want to. I hadn't since that dinner when everything felt too intense. Again.

But I looked anyway.

His eyes searched my face. "When's the last time you slept?"

"I slept fine."

"That's not what I asked." He took a protein bar out of his pocket and held it out to me without speaking.

I unwrapped it, grateful he didn't make a thing out of it.

I took a bite and another drink of coffee, then walked to the next row. Behind me, I heard him sigh.

The crew arrived as the sun broke over the hills. Eight men my father had known forever.

When they got to work, I grabbed shears and a bin and headed into the first row.

Snapper followed.

The vines were planted close enough together that we had to work single file, passing the bins forward as they filled. Cut, lay, move, repeat. My hands knew the work without thinking. Which was good, because thinking about what I was doing, why I was doing it, what would happen if this didn't work, made each breath take effort.

"Hand me that bin," Snapper said from behind me.

I did.

"You've been avoiding me," he said.

"I haven't." I cut three more clusters and laid them in the bin. "We're harvesting. Can we not do this right now?"

"Do what?"

"Talk about things that don't matter."

Silence. Then so quiet I almost didn't hear it: "I didn't realize I didn't matter."

I caught myself before I crushed the cluster in my hand when my shears slipped. "That's not what I meant."

"Then, what did you mean?"

"Not that," I said under my breath.

We worked without talking after that. The only sounds were the shears snipping, the leaves rustling, and the low conversations from the crew in other rows. My back started to ache, and my hands cramped. The sun climbed higher, and sweat soaked through my shirt.

By midmorning, I'd changed into a tank top and still couldn't cool down. I grabbed a water bottle from the cooler at the end of the row and drained half of it.

Snapper appeared beside me, reaching for his own bottle. His shirt was damp too, sticking to his chest and shoulders. He lifted the bottle to drink, and I watched his throat work as he swallowed.

"Have you eaten today?" he blurted.

"I'm not hungry."

"I didn't ask if you were hungry." He stepped closer. "I asked when you last ate."

"Yesterday. Maybe. I don't know." I scrubbed a hand over my face. "Does it matter?"

"Yeah, it matters." His jaw tightened. "You're running yourself into the ground."

"I'm fine."

"Quit saying that. You're not fine. You've got shadows under your eyes. You've lost weight. Your hands are shaking."

I looked down. He was right. My hands trembled against my thighs.

"You need to rest."

"I can't." The words came out sharper than I intended. "I can't stop. I can't—" The rest of what I was about to say stuck in my throat.

Snapper reached up and cupped my cheek. His touch was gentle enough to make my eyes burn. "Saff—"

"We should get to work." I stepped away and headed toward the vines.

I felt his gaze on my back, but he didn't follow immediately.

The afternoon was brutal. Heat pressed down, and my exhaustion made everything harder. I dropped a cluster, stumbled between vines, and forgot to move my bin forward, so I had to backtrack.

Every time, Snapper was there, steadying me. Moving my bin without comment.

By five o'clock, we'd picked the last cluster, and the bins were loaded onto the truck that would take them straight to Los Caballeros.

My hands shook harder as I watched the purple-black fruit disappear.

"Saff," he said quietly. "Go inside."

"I need to help—"

"We've got it."

"But—"

"Please." He stepped closer, and I saw the concern in his eyes. "Let us handle getting the fruit into the tanks."

I thanked him, then went inside the house that felt too big and empty. I showered and changed into pajama pants and an oversized sweatshirt that used to be my dad's. Then I sat at the kitchen table with a glass of water I didn't drink.

The mail was stacked in the center of the table. Bills I couldn't pay. Notices I'd been ignoring.

I opened the top envelope. Equipment supplier. Past due. Please remit.

The next one was from our wine distributor. Account suspended. Outstanding balance must be paid.

I set them aside and reached for the next. And the next. Each one worse than the last.

My vision blurred as tears spilled down my cheeks before I could stop them.

I couldn't fall apart. Not now.

But my body didn't listen. The sobs came anyway—ugly, choking sounds that hurt. I pressed my hands over my face but couldn't stop.

Days of holding it together had taken their toll on me. I couldn't do this anymore. Couldn't carry it alone. Couldn't be strong enough or smart enough to save us. I was going to fail, and we were going to lose everything.

Headlights swept across the kitchen window.

I heard a truck door slam. Footsteps on the porch. A knock.

"Saff? You in there?"

I couldn't answer through the sobs.

He opened the door I'd forgotten to lock.

"Jesus, Saff—"

Snapper crossed the kitchen and dropped to his knees beside my chair. His hands framed my face, turning me toward him.

I couldn't look at him. Couldn't let him see me breaking.

"I can't do this anymore."

"Can't do what?"

"Any of it. All of it." I shook my head, pulling away from his hands. "I'm so tired."

"Then, rest."

"I can't." Another sob tore through me. "If I stop, if I rest, if I let go for even a second—"

"What? What happens if you let go?"

"We lose everything."

Snapper went still. "The foreclosure."

I looked up. "You knew?"

"I heard rumors. How bad is it?"

Everything poured out of me. The call from the bank. The threat that if we didn't bring the account current, they'd begin foreclosure.

"That's why I needed the favor," I said. "Why I needed your family's grapes and equipment. Why the wine has to work. This is the only chance." My voice broke. "And what if it doesn't work? What if I fail? What if I lose everything anyway?"

Silence stretched between us. I waited for him to tell me I should've trusted him sooner. That I'd made everything worse.

Instead, he said, "Okay."

I blinked. "Okay?"

"Okay. We make the wine. We save the winery."

"Snapper—"

"You're not alone, Saffron. You hear me?"

"You don't understand how much money—"

"I don't care about the money. I care about you."

"But—"

"Listen to me." His intensity made me go still. "We have what we need. The wine is going to work. And if it doesn't, we'll figure out another way. But you're done carrying this alone." He sighed. "And that's another thing. I want you to know that I get why you don't want your dad to know."

"You do?"

"Yes. He'd never accept the help, and not because he wouldn't appreciate it. His pride…"

I was crying again, but I felt lighter. My chest loosened. My shoulders dropped. Air came easier.

"I'm so tired," I whispered.

"I know."

"I've been so scared."

"I know, sweetheart. I know."

He put his arms around me, and I curled into his chest. One of his hands slid into my hair, and I buried my face against his shoulder.

"We'll figure it out," he murmured against my hair. "I promise."

I believed him, finally accepting that maybe letting someone help didn't make me weak. Maybe it just made me human.

My breathing evened out, and the tears stopped.

When I rested my hand on his chest, his shirt was damp beneath it. "Sorry."

"Don't be." He moved the hair back from my face. "Feel better?"

"A little." I let out a shaky laugh. "I'm still terrified."

"That's fair." His thumb traced along my cheekbone.

"Thank you," I whispered.

"For what?"

"For being here. For not leaving when you saw what a mess I am."

"Saff." He waited until I looked at him. "I'm not going anywhere. I've told you that so often you're probably sick of hearing it, but I mean it."

The way he looked at me made my pulse kick up. Not from fear this time. From want.

His gaze dropped to my eyes, then to my mouth. The air between us shifted.

"Saffron…"

"Yeah?"

"Tell me to leave."

"Why would I do that?"

"Because if I stay—" He stopped. Swallowed. "If I stay, I'm going to kiss you. And I don't think I'll be able to stop at just kissing."

My heart hammered against my ribs. "I don't want you to stop."

His eyes darkened. "You need to be sure."

"I am sure. I need you to stay. I need to be with you."

His hands slid from my face down to my waist, and I rose up on my toes to kiss him.

He made a sound low in his throat and brought me closer. His mouth was warm and demanding.

His hands moved to my hips, then lower, gripping my thighs as he lifted me. I wrapped my legs around his waist, and he pressed me against the wall, kissing me like he'd been starving for it.

"Upstairs," I gasped against his mouth.

He leaned away enough to look at me, checking, making sure before he carried me toward the stairs.

13

Snapper

At the top of the stairs, I set her down outside her bedroom door. She swayed, and I put my hands on her waist to steady her. Even now, after everything she'd just told me, after she'd let me in, I had to be sure.

"You okay with this?"

She pulled my mouth back to hers. The kiss was slower this time, deeper, and when I stared into them, her eyes were clear. "I've never been more sure of anything."

Inside her room, I took in the details I'd never seen before. Books stacked on the nightstand—technical volumes about viticulture mixed with travel guides for places she'd never visited but said she wanted to. A quilt, probably from her grandmother, that looked handmade, was draped across the bed.

She stood beside it, twisting her hands together.

I stepped closer and cupped her face. "We can stop anytime."

"I don't want to stop." Her hands rested on my chest. "I want this. I want you."

She reached for the hem of my shirt, and I helped her pull it over my head. Her hands explored my chest, her fingers tracing muscle and the rope-burn scar on my ribs from a tussle with a steer a few years ago. When she reached my shoulder, her touch gentled.

"Does it hurt?"

"Not right now." I caught her hand and kissed her palm. "Right now, I don't feel anything but you."

I found the buttons of her shirt and worked them slowly, watching her face flush as each one came free. When I pushed it off her shoulders, I saw what I'd imagined for years—tan lines from working in the vineyard, her shoulders darker than the pale skin below. Freckles scattered across her collarbone like someone had splattered wine across marble.

"You're so damn beautiful," I said, tracing the line where sun-kissed skin met pale.

More clothes came off. Then I unzipped her jeans covered with faint purple stains that wouldn't wash out completely. Her hands were callused from the pruning shears, and her cuticles were also stained despite scrubbing.

I lay her on the bed and followed her down, settling my weight carefully over her. The first touch of skin to skin made us both gasp.

I kissed her deeply, taking my time. My hands learned her body—the dip of her waist, the curve of her hip, the softness of her breasts. When I traced my thumb across her nipple and felt it harden, she arched beneath me.

"Snapper, please—"

"I've got you." I kissed down her neck, across her collarbone, and lower. When I took her nipple in my mouth, her fingers tightened in my hair and she made a sound that shot straight to my cock.

Now, I had her beneath me, trusting me with her body after trusting me with her truth, and I was going to make damn sure she never regretted it.

My mouth continued making its way down her stomach, feeling her muscles jump under my lips. When I settled between her thighs, she tensed.

"Relax, sweetheart. Let me take care of you."

I put my mouth on her, and her hips lifted off the bed. I took my time, learning what made her moan, what made her hands fist in the sheets, what made her say my name. When she came against my tongue, I memorized the taste of her.

I moved up her body, kissing her deeply so she could taste herself on my lips. Her hands were frantic, pulling at my shoulders, trying to get me closer.

"I need you," she gasped. "Please, I need—"

After rolling on the condom I'd taken from my wallet and set on the bedside table, I positioned myself and pushed inside her slowly. We both froze at the sensation—her hot and tight around me, me stretching her, filling her. Perfect.

When she moved her hips, I was lost.

We found a rhythm, like we'd been doing this for years instead of minutes. Her legs wrapped around my waist, and I laced my fingers through hers, pinning her hands beside her head. I watched her face—the way her lips parted the deeper I went, the flush spreading down her neck, the small crease between her brows when I changed the angle.

"Look at me," I said when her eyes started to drift closed. "I want to see you."

She held my gaze. No walls. No barriers.

I reached between us and touched her where we were joined. Her back arched, and she shattered, her body clenching around me in waves.

The sensation sent me over right after her. I buried my face in her neck and came hard, holding her.

I managed to roll to my back before my arms gave out and I crushed her with my weight. Her head rested on my chest and my fingers traced patterns up and down her spine.

"I never thought it could be like that," she whispered.

I tilted her face up. "Like what?"

"Safe and intense at the same time. Like coming home and jumping off a cliff."

I kissed her softly. "That's what it felt like for me too."

She settled against my chest again, resting her hand over my heart.

Soon, we both drifted to sleep.

When I woke, her eyes were open and her brow furrowed.

"Talk to me, Saffron."

When she shook her head, I crawled on top of her, using my arms to hold my weight. "Tell me what's going on?"

Her eyes bored into mine. "What if the wine doesn't work?"

"It will."

"But what if it doesn't? What if we do everything right, and it's still not good enough?" Her fingers traced circles on my arms. "What if December comes, and we open those tanks, and it's…ordinary?"

I rolled to my side and brought her with me so her body was stretched on top of mine. "Then we'll figure something else out."

"There is nothing else, Snapper. This is it. This is the only chance."

"Saff." I reached up and cupped her cheek so she had to look at me. "You're borrowing trouble. Right now, we've got everything we need. That's enough."

She was quiet for several seconds. "I keep thinking about the journal entry. How they agreed to split the formula. 'What we created can never be made again.' What if they were right?"

"Or what if something happened we'll never know about or understand that kept them from making it again? Sometimes, the only thing stopping us from fixing a problem is our own stubbornness."

She huffed but smiled. "Are you saying I'm stubborn?"

"I'm saying you come by it honest." I kissed her forehead. "But at least now, you've got backup."

"Yeah. I do." She settled against me again. "Thank you. For staying. For listening. For not trying to fix everything the second I told you about the foreclosure."

"You don't need me to fix it. You need me to help you fix it. There's a difference."

"Is there?"

"Yeah. One makes you feel weak. The other makes you stronger."

Her breathing evened out, and the tension in her body slowly released.

"Try to sleep," I murmured.

"Will you stay?"

"All night. I'm not going anywhere."

She relaxed against me, and within minutes, she was asleep with her head on my chest and her body flush with mine. I couldn't imagine a better feeling in the world, other than being inside of her. There'd be plenty of time for that later. For the rest of our lives if I had anything to say about it.

I stayed awake longer, staring at the ceiling. Eventually, I drifted off too.

The alarm at five AM jolted us both awake. Saffron stirred and groaned in protest, then she stilled.

She rolled to face me. "Hi," she whispered.

"Hi, yourself."

"You stayed."

"Told you I would."

She kissed me, soft and slow, but when she leaned away, I saw the question in her eyes—did last night change things between us?

I kissed her back, deeper this time. Yeah, everything had changed. For the better.

"We need to pick today," she said against my mouth.

"I know."

"So we should—"

I tightened my arms around her. "Five more minutes."

She settled into me with a sigh. "Five more minutes."

They stretched into ten, then fifteen. Neither of us wanted to move.

She got up first. "I really do need to shower. The crew will be waiting."

"Go ahead. I'll make coffee."

"You don't know where anything is."

"I have mad skills as a hunter and gatherer, sweetheart, which means I can sniff out coffee anywhere."

She rolled her eyes, smiled, and climbed out of bed. I watched her walk to the bathroom, appreciating every curve and line of her body that I now knew intimately.

She paused in the doorway and looked back at me. "You could join me."

"If I do that, we'll never make it to the vineyard."

Her laugh echoed off the bathroom tiles as she disappeared inside. A minute later, I heard the water start.

I forced myself out of bed, put on my jeans, and headed downstairs. The coffeemaker sat on the counter next to the sink. I found grounds in the freezer and filters in the same cabinet as the cups.

While the coffee brewed, I looked around. There was mail stacked on the table and a calendar on the wall that had harvest dates marked in red, but I noticed the ink was smudged in places, like she'd erased and rewritten dates multiple times. There was a photo on the refrigerator of Saffron and Felicity, probably from five years ago, both of them laughing at something outside the frame.

The kitchen window looked out over the Zinfandel vines we'd harvested yesterday, now stripped of fruit.

When the coffeemaker beeped, I poured two mugs and carried them upstairs.

She was just coming out of the bathroom, wrapped in a towel, hair damp and smelling like citrus and honey. She took the mug I offered and sipped, then smiled.

"Perfect. Thank you."

She set it down, then kissed me. "Your turn to shower. I'll get dressed and check the weather."

I kissed her forehead and went into the bathroom. The small space still smelled like her—not just her shampoo, but something else, something that was purely Saffron. I showered quickly, knowing daylight was fast approaching, then dressed in yesterday's clothes.

When I came downstairs, she was in the kitchen, wearing clean jeans and a Los Caballeros T-shirt I recognized as one of mine from a harvest party two years ago. Seeing her in it made my chest tight.

"That looks better on you than it ever did on me," I said.

She glanced down. "Oh. I forgot I had this. I can change—"

"Don't you dare." I put my arms around her and ran my hands down her back. "I like seeing you in my clothes. It means you're mine."

"Possessive much?"

"When it comes to you? Yeah."

She rose up on her toes and kissed me, and I could taste coffee and toothpaste and home.

She stepped away and grabbed her phone from the counter. "I checked the forecast. Clear today and tomorrow, but there's a system coming in on Saturday. Rain."

"How much?"

"Enough to make a mess if we're still picking." She opened the weather app and showed me. "Looks like it'll hit late afternoon. We need everything off the vines and into the tanks by then."

"It'll happen."

"If nothing goes wrong."

"When does anything go wrong during harvest?" I deadpanned.

That got a genuine laugh from her. "Fair point."

I took out my phone and texted my brothers, making sure the crew was on schedule. A response came back immediately from Bit, saying they'd already gotten started.

"Should we leave now?" she asked.

"In a sec." I kissed her one more time, then grabbed my keys and phone and headed for the door.

Outside, the October morning was cool and clear, the kind of day that made you grateful to be alive and working in wine country. I opened the passenger door of my truck, and she climbed in, then I got behind the wheel.

Saffron sat beside me and reached over to put her hand in mine.

"Nervous?" I asked as we got close.

"Terrified," she admitted. "But in a good way. Maybe."

I glanced at her and smiled. "That's honest."

"I'm trying to be." She squeezed my hand. "About everything."

"I know you are."

I drove through the gates of Los Caballeros just as the sun broke over the eastern hills, turning the vineyard rows to gold. Like Bit had said, the crew was already there—trucks were lined up, bins were stacked and ready, and Cru was checking his clipboard.

I put the truck in park and looked at Saffron. "Ready?"

She studied me—this man who'd been her friend for years, who'd become her lover last night, who was now helping her fight to save everything that mattered.

"Ready."

As I climbed out of the truck and went around to open her door, a feeling of foreboding settled in my gut like none I'd ever felt before. I just prayed it had nothing to do with the grapes we were about to pick or the wine that Saffron's family's future depended on.

14

Saffron

I stood on the crush pad at Los Caballeros, watching the last bin of Syrah grapes get hoisted toward the tank. Beside me, Snapper's hand found mine, and he laced our fingers together like we'd been doing it for years instead of days.

"That's the last of it," Cru called from the catwalk above the tanks. "We're looking at enough fruit for fifteen hundred bottles minimum."

Fifteen hundred bottles. Fifteen hundred chances to save everything.

Bit appeared at my shoulder, clipboard in hand. "Whole clusters going in now. CO2 injection in five minutes."

I watched the grapes disappear into the sealed tanks. Six to eight weeks of waiting while the wine did what we couldn't control.

"Are your parents still in Napa?" Eberly asked.

"Yeah. Felicity's baby isn't ready to come out yet, I guess."

I stood staring at the tanks. Inside them, our future was either being saved or I was about to fail spectacularly in front of both our families and our closest friends. The weight of it pressed down on my shoulders. And my parents had no idea any of this was happening.

"Now, we wait," Cru said, moving between monitors.

"You've done your part." Daphne removed her work gloves. "Let the wine do its work now."

Snapper's arm slid around my waist. "Hear that? Time for us to take a break and let the juice cook."

I looked up at him. He had grape must on his jaw, and his hair was a mess, and I wanted to kiss him right there in front of everyone. The urge hit so hard I had to look away before I acted on it.

"Come on." He steered me toward the parking lot. "I need food and a shower."

Behind us, I heard Bit say something to Eberly that made her laugh. When I glanced back, they were both watching us.

"They know," I said when we reached his truck.

"Of course they do." He opened my door. "Bit's been aware of how I felt about you for years. Pretty sure everyone is by now."

Heat flooded my cheeks. "That obvious?"

"Yeah." He kissed me, slow and deep, right where anyone could see us. When he leaned away, his eyes had gone dark. "Dinner tonight?"

"Your place or mine?"

"Yours. I'll cook."

I drove home exhausted but too wired to rest. I showered until the water ran cool, washing away three days of harvest work.

My phone buzzed as I was getting dressed. *Miss you already.*

I smiled despite my exhaustion. *You just saw me twenty minutes ago.*

Still miss you.

The next two weeks fell into a rhythm. Snapper and I stayed together most nights—sometimes at my place, sometimes his. We'd collapse into bed exhausted from commercial harvest work and wake up tangled together, neither of us wanting to move.

Small arguments cropped up. He left socks everywhere. I used all the hot water. We'd bicker and make up, and I'd find myself thinking this was what a life together looked like. The mundane mixed with the profound.

"What happens after all the wine is sold?" I asked one night in late October. We were at his place, both too tired to do anything but lie in bed. His fingers traced lazy patterns on my bare shoulder.

"What do you want to happen?"

"I don't know." I pressed my face against his chest. "I'm afraid to think that far ahead."

His hand stilled. "Maybe that's the problem. Maybe we should think about it."

"Like what?"

"This being permanent."

My heart kicked against my ribs. "Is that what you want?"

"Yeah, Saff. That's exactly what I want."

"We hardly know each other. I mean, we know each other, but not that way. I mean—"

"I've wanted you for years, Saffron Hope." He tucked hair behind my ear. "But I'm not pushing. I'm just saying—when you're ready to think about the future, I'll be way ahead of you."

I kissed him instead of answering. His arms came around me, and I let myself get lost in the feel of him, in the solid reality of his body against mine.

Halloween fell on a Friday. I met Snapper at his house just as the sun was dropping toward the horizon. His driveway was packed with vehicles, including Tryst and Jaicon's SUV, Brix and Addy's truck, and Alex and Maddox's minivan with its collection of car seats.

"Fair warning," he said when I climbed out. "My family goes all out for this."

"I remember. Your mom used to give out full-size candy bars."

"Still does." He took my hand and led me inside. "She buys them in bulk from Costco."

Chaos greeted us. Kids in costumes ran everywhere—Tryst and Jaicon's daughter, Neva, dressed as a butterfly with gossamer wings, Brix and Addy's daughter, Reagan, as a dinosaur complete with tail, Alex and

Maddox's daughter, Coco, as a winemaker, complete with fake grapes sewn all around her purple-stained jeans. Alfonso was a baseball player. Lucia stood in the middle of it all like a general coordinating troops.

"Snapper!" She shouted when she spotted us. "You're on candy duty at your house tonight. The bowl is already there."

He saluted. "Yes, ma'am."

"And, Saffron!" She gathered me in a hug before I could brace for it. "So good to see you, *mija*. You look tired. Are you eating enough?"

"I'm fine—"

"She's been working harvest," Snapper said. "We both have."

Before Lucia could interrogate me further, Reagan barreled into my legs with the force of a small meteor. "*Tía* Saffron!"

What she'd called me hit me square in the chest. *Tía.* It was Spanish for aunt and used like I already belonged to this family.

I froze, looking down at her little dinosaur face. She grinned up at me, completely oblivious to the way she'd just cracked something open inside me.

Snapper's eyes met mine across the mayhem. His smile was soft and understanding.

"Hey, Reagan." I crouched down to her level. "You're a very scary dinosaur."

She roared, showing me all her teeth. I pretended to be terrified, throwing my hands up. She giggled and ran off to terrorize someone else, her tail bouncing behind her.

Snapper watched as I slowly straightened, and something in his expression made my chest tight. Like he was seeing a future I was too afraid to imagine.

"You okay?" he asked quietly.

"Yeah. Just—" I glanced at Reagan disappearing into the kitchen. "*Tía.* That's a big word."

"She's three. She doesn't know it's big." His hand felt warm on my lower back when he wrapped me in his arms. "But yeah. It is."

We spent the evening handing out candy while the parents and kids trick-or-treated through the neighborhood. The streets were packed with families, porch lights blazing, the air filled with excited shouts and laughter. I held Snapper's hand as we greeted each visitor and held out the tub of candy for them to choose from. As they came and went, kids compared their haul while parents chatted about school and sports and whose turn it was to host Thanksgiving.

When we ran out of our stash, we turned off the porch light and went in search of the others. I watched Snapper adjust Neva's butterfly wings so they wouldn't get crushed before hoisting her onto his shoulders when she got tired. I marveled at the way he and the kids pointed at decorations, and how animated he was when they argued over which was the best.

This was who he'd be with our kids someday.

The thought came unbidden, and I nearly stumbled. *Our kids.* When had I started thinking in terms of *our* anything?

"You good?" He glanced over his shoulder at me, Neva's little hands gripping his hair.

"Yeah. Just tripped."

But I wasn't good. I was watching him with a two-year-old on his shoulders and imagining a future where we did this with our own children. Where I wasn't just *Tía* Saffron but Mom. Where he was Dad and we had a house full of chaos and candy and little feet running everywhere.

The image was so vivid it hurt. Because none of it could happen if the wine didn't work. If we lost the winery. If I failed.

When we returned to his house, where the kids were hyped on sugar and the adults exhausted, I sat on his couch with his arm around me. The house smelled like chocolate, and autumn leaves tracked in on small feet. Reagan had crashed on Addy's lap. Neva was showing her butterfly wings to anyone who would look.

Alex appeared from the kitchen with two beers, handing one to me before dropping into the chair across from us. "So," she said, her eyes sparkling with mischief. "You two are finally ready to admit you're more than just friends?"

Heat flooded my face. "Alex—"

"About damn time." She grinned. "I've been watching you two dance around each other since high school. Thought I'd die of old age before you figured it out."

Snapper laughed. "Nice, sis."

"I'm just saying." When he got up and disappeared into another room, Alex took a sip of her beer, then her expression softened. "He's happy, Saff. Really happy. I haven't seen him like this ever." She paused, studying me. "You're happy too, right? Because you deserve this."

"I am," I said quietly. "Happy, I mean."

"Good." She reached over and squeezed my knee. "Then, don't mess it up by overthinking everything like you always do. Just let yourself have this."

Snapper returned from wherever he'd gone and dropped beside me onto the couch, pulling me against his side. Alex winked at me before rejoining Maddox across the room.

I watched Snapper laugh at something Tryst said and listened to him tease his nieces with gentle affection.

What Alex had said echoed in my head. *Don't mess it up by overthinking everything. Just let yourself have this.*

I wanted to. God, I wanted to. But letting myself have things had never come easily to me.

The call came on a Thursday morning in early November. I was at the kitchen table, staring at bills we couldn't pay, when my phone rang.

"Honey, the doctor is inducing labor today." My mom sounded excited but equally anxious. "The baby is measuring big, and the doctor doesn't want to wait any longer. They're prepping Felicity now."

I sat up straight. "I am on my way. I will get there as soon as I can."

"Perfect. Text me when you know your arrival time."

After we hung up, I texted Snapper. *Mom just called. They are inducing labor today. I'm flying to Napa.*

His response came immediately. *Good. Your sister needs you. I'll keep an eye on things here.*

I went to the airline website and found a seat on the next available departure. Within an hour, I had clothes thrown in a bag and was driving to the airport. By early afternoon, I was on a plane heading north.

I took a car service from the airport straight to the hospital. My dad was in the waiting room, pacing and checking his phone. He wrapped me in a tight hug when he saw me.

"I am so glad you're here."

"Where's Mom?"

"She is with Felicity and Wagner. They are only letting two people back at a time."

The hours crawled by. While Dad paced, I sat and tried not to think about the wine fermenting four hundred miles away. There was nothing I could do about it anyway. Bit and Cru had it covered.

Mom came out periodically with updates. "She's doing great. Progressing well. It shouldn't be too much longer."

At six-thirty in the evening, Wagner appeared in the doorway, looking exhausted but elated.

"It is a girl," he said. "Eight pounds, six ounces. Felicity did great. We named her Beatrice Diane."

Relief flooded through me. Dad teared up, and I embraced Wagner.

"Can we see them?" Dad asked.

"Soon. They're just getting cleaned up. But—" Wagner's expression shifted. "The pediatrician heard a heart murmur. They're running tests."

The relief evaporated. "What does that mean?"

"They don't know yet. It could be nothing—lots of babies have murmurs that resolve on their own. It could also mean she needs surgery. They're monitoring her overnight and doing an echocardiogram tomorrow morning."

Dad's hand found my shoulder and gripped tight.

We stayed at Felicity and Wagner's house that night. The guest room I was in was comfortable, but I doubted I'd sleep much. How would any of us, not knowing what tomorrow would bring?

Around nine, I called Snapper. He picked up on the first ring.

"Hey. How's it going?"

"Felicity and Wagner had a baby girl. She's eight pounds, six ounces. But she has a heart murmur."

"Jesus, Saff. Is that bad? I mean, it sounds bad."

"Not sure. They're running tests. It could be nothing, or it could mean she needs surgery." I sat on the edge of the guest bed, staring at the wall. "Wagner looked terrified. Felicity is trying to be strong, but she is falling apart."

"How are you?"

"Scared. Tired. Wishing you were here."

The admission came out before I could stop it.

"I can be on a plane in an hour," he said. "It'll put me there by midnight."

"No. You need to stay there. The wine—"

"The wine is fine. It is just sitting in tanks. Bit and Cru have it covered."

"I know. But—"

"But what?"

"It is complicated."

Another pause. Then, "Okay. But if you need me, I'm there. One phone call, and I'm on my way."

"I know. Thank you."

"Will you call me tomorrow after the tests?"

"I will."

After we hung up, I lay in the dark and let myself cry. I cried for Beatrice and for Felicity. I cried because I wanted Snapper here so badly it hurt.

The next morning, the tests confirmed that Beatrice had a ventricular septal defect—a hole in the wall between the lower chambers of her heart. It was not immediately life-threatening, but it was serious enough to require surgical repair.

They scheduled the operation for the following Tuesday. Five days from now. Five days to wait and try not to imagine all the things that could go wrong.

I texted Snapper constant updates. He immediately replied, steadying me even though he was four hundred miles away.

How are you holding up? he asked Saturday night.

I'm okay. Scared. I sat in the guest room at Felicity's house, staring at my phone. *Beatrice is so tiny. The surgery seems huge.*

She is tougher than she looks. She gets it from her aunt.

How is the wine doing?

It is fine. Do not worry about it.

I am trying not to.

I miss you, I typed.

I miss you too, sweetheart.

Tuesday morning arrived gray and cold. We convened in the surgical waiting room at six in the morning—Mom, Dad, Wagner's parents, and me. Wagner and Felicity were with Beatrice, at least until the surgery started. Then they'd be in another waiting room just for the parents.

The doctor told my sister that the surgery could take as long as six hours. I couldn't fathom that. Six hours to open her tiny chest, repair a valve in her heart, and close her back up.

I texted Snapper to say the surgery was about to start.

His response came immediately. *She is going to be perfect. Just like her aunt.*

I held onto those words like a lifeline.

The first hour crawled by. No news. That was normal, they'd said. We would only hear if something went wrong.

Felicity came out to where we waited, saying she needed to be with her family, then paced, unable to sit still. Wagner stayed near her, murmuring things I couldn't hear. My mom prayed, her lips moving silently. Dad stared at the television mounted in the corner, not really watching.

I texted Snapper. *One hour down.*

It's gonna go great. I know it.

At hour two, a new family came in. Their daughter was having her tonsils out. The mother was chatty, nervous, trying to fill the silence with small talk. I wanted to scream at her that tonsils were not the same as open-heart surgery. That her daughter would be fine and my sister's might not be. But I couldn't think that way, let alone say it.

Two hours in, there still wasn't any news.

My chest felt tight, compressed. Every time the door opened, we all turned as one, with our hearts in our throats, but it was never someone looking for us.

At hour three, Felicity broke down. "It has been too long. Something's wrong."

"They said six hours," Wagner reminded her.

"What if…?" Tears streamed down my sister's face.

My mom wrapped her arms around her. "Beatrice is going to be fine, Felicity. The doctors are making sure of it."

"You don't know…"

"I do know." Mom spoke quietly but fiercely. "I know it because she is a Staglin and a Hope, and we do not give up. She is going to fight, and she is going to win."

I texted Snapper. *Felicity is falling apart.*

Be there for her. That is all you can do. You're doing great.

But I wasn't. I was sitting in a waiting room while my infant niece's chest was cracked open, while surgeons worked on a heart so small it seemed impossible to fix.

I thought about her little fists, how her fingers had curled around mine when I had held her hand through the NICU isolette. I thought about how she had opened her eyes once, just for a second, and seemed to look right at me.

I thought about Snapper hoisting Neva onto his shoulders at Halloween. I thought about Reagan calling me *Tía*. I thought about the future I'd imagined—the one with kids and chaos and candy.

What if Beatrice never got to trick-or-treat? What if she never got to be three years old? What if this was it—I got up and walked out of the waiting room. I couldn't let Felicity see me fall apart, not when I was supposed to be here for her.

At hour five and a half, my hands were shaking. Felicity had stopped crying and gone silent, which was worse. Dad and Wagner both paced, and my mom's lips still moved in silent prayer.

Wagner's mother kept checking her watch like she could speed time up through sheer force of will.

I did too. When six hours came and went, I felt like I'd crawl out of my skin. Where was the surgeon? Why hadn't he come out yet?

At six hours and forty-five minutes, the door opened.

We all stood in a semicircle around the surgeon, my sister, and brother-in-law.

"The surgery was successful," he said, and the relief that swept through the room was physical.

Wagner caught Felicity when her knees buckled, and my parents and Wagner's both hugged.

I stood shaking, wiping away tears as fast as they fell.

"We were able to repair the defect," the surgeon continued. "She did very well. Better than expected, actually. She's in recovery now. Strong vitals. No complications."

He gave us more details—Beatrice's heart was pumping properly, but she would be in the NICU for a few days.

After he left, I texted Snapper with trembling fingers. *She made it through. She is okay.*

Call me, Saff.

I stepped out into the hall and pressed the speed dial for him. "Hey," I said when he answered.

"God, it's good to hear your voice. How are you?"

Exhausted. Grateful. Wrung out. Relieved beyond measure. "I'm okay. I miss you."

"I miss you too, sweetheart. Tell me you want me to come and I'll be on the way."

I said I would and that I'd call him again later, once we were back at the house.

When I returned to the waiting room, Felicity and Wagner weren't there.

"The doctor said they could see her," my mom explained.

Ten minutes later, the door opened and my sister motioned to me. "Bea needs to see her godmother," she said, wrapping her arm through mine as she led me into the NICU.

"You can touch her," Felicity said.

I reached through the isolette and laid my hand on her tiny arm. "Hey, Beatrice," I whispered. "You did so good. You're so strong."

Her eyes opened, just for a second. Dark eyes, unfocused but there.

Tears streamed down my cheeks, but I smiled.

Felicity hugged me. "Thank you for being here."

"Where else would I be?"

The days that followed blurred into a routine of morning visits to the hospital, then helping Felicity, who was recovering from childbirth while trying to be strong for her daughter. I ran errands, got food, and tried to be useful in whatever way I could.

How's the wine? I texted Snapper one evening.

Good. Bit says we are on track.

I should be there.

You are exactly where you need to be.

He periodically sent photos of the wine tanks with their blinking monitors. His truck parked at the winery. Normal things. Reminders that life was continuing without me.

I sent photos back. Beatrice improving, growing. My parents smiling. Felicity holding her daughter.

We talked every night. It was the only thing that made the separation bearable.

"I wish you were here," I said one night, lying in bed.

"I wish I was too."

One afternoon, I was alone in Beatrice's room while Felicity napped and my parents grabbed lunch. I sat in the rocking chair, holding my niece for the first time since her surgery.

She was so light in my arms. So fragile. The incision on her chest was covered with gauze and surgical tape. She made little snuffling sounds in her sleep.

I started humming without thinking. An old lullaby my grandmother used to sing. The melody came back to me like muscle memory.

Beatrice's eyes opened, and she looked up at me.

"Hey, sweet girl," I whispered. "You are so brave."

Her little mouth opened wide, and she yawned. Then she settled against my chest, her ear over my heart.

I sat there, rocking her, humming, feeling her breathe. And I thought about the future. I thought about Snapper hoisting kids onto his shoulders. I thought about Thanksgiving dinners and Christmas mornings. I thought about a life that included this—babies and family and love so fierce it was terrifying.

I wanted it. God, I wanted it. All of it.

But before I could, I needed to make sure our family didn't lose everything.

Beatrice continued improving daily, and the doctors were optimistic about discharge within the week—just in time for Thanksgiving. And that meant I could go home soon too.

15

I was tossing my duffel bag into the passenger seat of my truck when Kick appeared in my driveway, coffee mug in hand and that shit-eating grin already plastered across his face.

"So," he said, lifting his foot to rest on my front bumper. "You're driving four hours to surprise your girlfriend on the day before Thanksgiving."

"That's the plan."

"Without telling her you're coming."

"That's what makes it a surprise, genius." I moved around to the driver's side, but he followed.

"What if she doesn't want you there?"

The question stung more than I wanted to admit. I'd been asking myself the same thing for the past two days, ever since Diana had called with the idea. "Then I'll turn around and drive back."

"Bullshit." Kick took a sip of coffee. "You're gone on her, Snap."

I didn't argue. Couldn't.

"She loves you too, you know?"

"You think?" I opened the truck door but didn't climb in yet.

"Anyone with eyes can see it. You two have been circling each other for years. Only difference now is you got your heads out of your asses long enough to do something about it."

I smiled despite myself. "Thanks for the vote of confidence."

"I'm serious." He straightened, his expression shifting to something more genuine. "You and Saffron? You're meant to be. You always have been. So, quit overthinking it, and go get your girl."

"What about Ma? Think she'll be mad I'm missing dinner with the family?"

"She will be if you don't tell her you're gonna miss it."

I rolled my eyes. "I planned to stop by on my way out of town."

Kick waved a hand. "Then, you're good. She won't care. I mean, I've always been her favorite anyway."

"Keep telling yourself that."

"It's true, and you know it." He grinned again. "Now, get out of here before you hit traffic."

I climbed into the truck and started the engine. Kick stepped back, raising his mug in salute. "Drive safe. Tell Saffron I said hi."

"Will do."

"And, Snap?" He waited until I looked at him. "Stop being scared. She's not going anywhere."

I backed out of the driveway and headed for my mother's house.

"I already know," she said as soon as I walked inside and found her in the kitchen.

"Fuckin' Kick," I muttered under my breath, just not quietly enough apparently since she smacked me with the spatula she had in her hand.

"Your brother didn't tell me. Diana did."

"Seriously?"

"She wanted to make sure I was okay with her 'stealing my son' away for the holiday. I told her you weren't my only son."

"Thanks, Ma. That's real nice."

She set the spatula on the counter and hugged me. "I will miss you, *mijo*, but I'm happier that you'll be with Saffron."

"Me too. I just hope she's happy about it."

My mother patted my cheek. "You should propose to her."

My eyes opened wide. "You don't think it's a little soon for that?"

When she picked up the spatula again, I backed away, which made her laugh. "You better get on the road, Salazar."

I kissed her cheek and left.

The drive gave me too much time to think.

Four hours alone with nothing but the road and my own head wasn't doing me any favors. I thought about what Kick had said. *You're meant to be. You always have been.*

I'd wanted to believe it for years. It was just easier said than done.

My phone buzzed with a text from Bit. *Wine update: carbonic maceration complete on all three varietals. Pressed yesterday. Alcoholic fermentation underway. Everything on schedule. Timeline still good for early December—seven weeks total from harvest. Should be ready to taste around the sixth or seventh.*

My chest loosened. That was good news. We were about five weeks in now, which meant it wouldn't be much longer before we'd know if the wine was what we needed it to be. We'd be cutting it close for bottling, labeling, and getting everything to auction by the deadline.

But it would work. It had to. And if it didn't, I had a Plan B. Not that Saffron would like it. I shook my head. Better not to think about that until the time came. *If* the time came, which I prayed it wouldn't.

My phone buzzed again. This time, it was Saffron. *Have a good Thanksgiving with your family. Miss you.*

Guilt twisted in my gut. Diana had insisted I not tell her about the surprise. "She needs this," she'd said when we planned it over the phone three days ago. "She's been so worried about the baby, about Felicity, about everything. Let her have this one good thing she's not expecting."

So I'd lied. Well, not lied, exactly. I just hadn't told her the whole truth.

You too. Miss you more, I texted back, though it felt inadequate. Three weeks apart felt like three months, and phone calls and texts weren't enough. Not even close. I missed her so much I had a permanent ache in my chest that wouldn't go away until I held her in my arms. Just thinking about the way she fit against me when we slept and the sound of her voice first thing in the morning made me wish I'd flown instead of driven.

I needed to be with her. Needed to hold her. Needed to make sure she was okay, because I wasn't convinced she was, not really. She'd been carrying too much for too long, and even though she'd told me about the foreclosure, I could still feel her pull away sometimes. Like she was afraid to need me too much.

I hadn't been on the road for more than thirty minutes when a call came in from Tryst.

"I understand we won't be seeing you at Thanksgiving today," he said after I accepted the call.

"I'm surprising Saffron in Napa."

"We will miss seeing you today, but I am happy to hear you'll be with her and her family. However, this is not the reason for my call. I wanted you to know I haven't had any luck identifying the woman named Ellen. A few remember hearing the name, but no one knows who she was or what happened."

"Thanks for the update, Tryst, and we'll catch up next week."

The news, while somewhat expected, unsettled me.

The rest of the drive was quiet, leaving me too much time alone with my thoughts. California's golden hillsides stretched out on either side of the highway. Every so often, I'd pass vineyards too. This time of year, they were mostly bare, the leaves gone and the vines pruned back for winter. Harvest was over everywhere. The grapes were in tanks or barrels, beginning their transformation.

I forced myself to stop stressing about the wine whose success was so important to Saffron. I had to stay positive. Believe it was the blessing the name said it was.

By the time I arrived at Wagner and Felicity's, the sun was low on the horizon and my nerves were shot. The house was beautiful. It was a two-story, modern farmhouse with plenty of space for a growing family. The Wagners had money, and it showed. Not in a flashy way, just in the solid, well-built way that came from generations of success in the wine business.

Diana must've been watching from the window because the front door opened before I'd even turned off the engine. I couldn't help but grin as I climbed out of the truck and she stepped onto the porch, finger pressed to her lips, shushing me.

"She's in the nursery, with the baby," Diana whispered when I reached her. "Felicity's resting."

"Where should I—"

"Go surprise her." Her eyes sparkled with mischief. "Upstairs, second door on the right."

I moved through the house as quietly as I could. Nice place. Warm. It felt like a family lived here. I could hear Saffron's singing as I climbed the stairs It was something I didn't recognize but knew it was off-key and sweet. The best part was she was completely unselfconscious about it. Like when she was stealing my food from my plate, Saffron had never been shy about singing at the top of her lungs, even when everyone around her gave her shit about not being able to carry a tune.

I stopped in the doorway of the nursery and watched her for a second. She sat in the rocking chair, with her niece cradled in her arms, backlit by the window. The baby was tiny, so small it made my chest ache. Saffron was lost in the moment, and I wished I could freeze time right there. Just hold onto this image of her forever.

"Pretty song. Should I recognize it?" I asked, winking.

She gasped, and her eyes went wide. *"Snapper?"*

She stood and moved toward me slowly, careful not to wake the baby I could now see was fast asleep.

"What are you—? How are you—?"

I crossed to her, unable to stop grinning. "Surprise," I whispered, kissing her.

"But you said—? Your family—?"

"I lied, but in my defense, your mom helped."

Her mouth gaped. "My mom knew?"

"And Felicity. It was their idea, but as soon as they mentioned it, I was all in."

She laughed and cried at the same time. "I'm so happy you're here."

I kissed her again. A second quick brush of lips because the baby was between us, but it was enough. Enough to ground me.

"I couldn't imagine spending Thanksgiving without you," I said against her mouth.

"I actually thought about surprising you. How crazy would that have been? Me there. You here."

The baby made a noise, and Saffron looked down at her with so much tenderness on her face it made my throat close.

"She's beautiful," I said.

"She really is." Saffron glanced up at me. "Want to hold her?"

"I— Yeah. Okay."

She transferred the tiny human into my arms, and I held my breath as I adjusted my grip. I'd held plenty of babies over the years—my nieces and nephews, friends' kids—but this was Saffron's niece. *Her* family. And the way she was watching me, the tenderness and vulnerability in her expression, made my heart swell.

"Hey there, *pequeña*," I murmured, gazing down at the little face. "I'm your *Tío* Snapper."

I looked up at Saffron, who had tears in her eyes. "I love that."

I raised a brow. "Not too soon?"

She smiled. "It wasn't too soon for your niece to call me *Tía*."

Downstairs, Wagner greeted me. We'd known each other for years—he was a good guy who made Felicity happy, which was all that mattered.

Lucas was the one who made me nervous. He came out of the kitchen, drying his hands on a dish towel, and when he saw me, his brow shot up.

"About time you showed up," he said. "Diana's been a nervous wreck."

We shook hands, the grip firm and familiar. Our families were intertwined—holidays, harvests, celebrations. But he was studying me differently now. Not as just another Avila kid, but as the man dating his daughter.

Diana appeared and herded everyone into the living room, insisting we all sit down and catch up. Wagner gave us the latest update on Beatrice. The surgery had gone perfectly, and the doctors were thrilled with her progress.

Felicity came down from upstairs, appearing tired but happy. "Thanks for coming. She's been moping."

"I have not been moping!" Saffron's face flushed.

"You've checked your phone approximately eight thousand times—a day."

Everyone laughed, and just like that, the tension eased. This was family. This was what I'd grown up with—the easy back-and-forth, the teasing, the comfortable way people who loved each other existed in the same space.

Except now I was here as Saffron's *boyfriend*, not just a family friend.

Conversations about how the harvests had gone flowed easily, as did stories about Beatrice, who had both her parents wrapped around her tiny finger already.

"You sticking around Paso or heading back to the circuit?" Lucas asked at one point.

"Staying. Done with rodeo."

His eyebrows went up. "That's new."

"Not that new. I've been thinking about it a while."

Next to me, Saffron's hand found mine. I squeezed her fingers and glanced over to find Diana smiling as she watched us.

After dinner, everyone headed to bed upstairs.

"We're in here," Saffron said, leading me into a guest room with windows that looked out over the vineyard.

"This is nice," I said, pulling her into my arms. "God, I missed you."

"I missed you too. So much that I decided if you changed your mind and went back to rodeo, I'd have to become a buckle bunny."

"You already are. My *only* buckle bunny."

"I better be."

Once we were in bed, she curled into my side and rested her head on my chest above my heart.

"So, is the wine really on schedule?" she asked after a few minutes of silence.

"Cru says it'll be ready to taste next week."

She tensed slightly, but I felt it.

"Hey." I held her closer. "It's going to be amazing."

"You keep saying that."

"Because I believe it."

She didn't answer, and I held her until her breathing evened out and she fell asleep.

I stayed awake longer, staring up at the darkness in the room, so happy she was in my arms for real rather than me just dreaming she was.

I woke early, like always. The house was still quiet except for the faint sound of a baby crying somewhere down the hall.

"I should check on her," Saffron said, rolling out the other side of the bed. "I volunteered to take the first shift today since I didn't know you were coming."

"What can I do?" I asked, watching as she put on a robe I immediately wanted to take off her just so I could look at her naked body a few minutes longer.

"Coffee, please." She practically groaned as she opened the door and eased out of the room.

Downstairs, I found Lucas already making a pot in the kitchen. We exchanged morning greetings, then just stood there, two men who'd known each other for years but had to navigate new territory now.

"She seems happy," he said, pouring coffee into three mugs. "Happier than I've seen her in a long time."

"I hope so."

"You serious about her?"

The question was direct, so I'd be equally so. "Yes, sir. Very serious."

"Good. She deserves someone who's all in."

"I am. All in. Maybe more than she is."

Diana appeared then, breaking the moment. "You two bonding?"

"Just talking, sweetheart," Lucas said, kissing her temple like I so often did with Saffron.

"I need to make a delivery," I said, pouring cream into the second mug and adding two heaping teaspoons of sugar.

"Just as she likes it," said Diana, watching me.

"I aim to please. Her especially."

That got me a smile from both her parents as I left the kitchen.

Once Wagner took over baby duty, Saffron and I went downstairs to help with breakfast prep—pancakes, eggs, bacon, sausage—just like it would be at my Ma's house on Thanksgiving morning. Except she'd also have chorizo.

Saffron and I moved around each other with the same ease we'd developed while together before she left to come up here. Each time we passed each other, I'd slip my arm around her waist and pull her in for a kiss.

I caught Lucas and Diana exchanging glances, but neither commented.

After breakfast and showers, Saffron and I went for a walk. The Napa morning was clear, cooler than down in our valley, but it felt good.

"Did my mom and Felicity really set this all up?" she asked as we walked hand in hand down the sidewalk.

"Yep. They like me."

She smiled. "You think so?"

I stopped walking. "Your dad asked if I was serious about you."

"What did you say?"

"That I'm all in."

She gazed up at me, searching my face. "Are you?"

"Absolutely, Saff. I really am."

I kissed her, long and deep, right there on the neighborhood corner, not caring who saw.

By midafternoon, the house smelled like Thanksgiving—turkey roasting, onions and celery sautéing for stuffing, and the sweet smell of pie crust baking. Everyone helped. Lucas managed the turkey with the focus of a man on a mission. Diana directed the side dishes while Felicity supervised from the living room, holding Beatrice and calling out instructions.

Wagner and I got stuck on mashed potato duty.

"So you and Saffron?" he said as he peeled another potato.

"Yep."

"About time."

I smiled despite myself. "That's what everyone keeps saying."

"Because it's true." He tossed the peeled potato into the pot. "You should know there's been a running bet about how long it would take you to make your move."

"Yeah? Who won?"

"Lemme think. Since we had to keep renewing it year after year, I guess Lucas got the closest."

"What did he win?"

Wagner nudged me with his shoulder. "I heard all he asked Santa for this year was another son-in-law."

"I hope to make his Christmas wish come true," I said. "Maybe not the wedding, but definitely the proposal."

Wagner dropped his knife on the counter, looked around to see who else was in earshot, then squeezed my shoulder. "I can't tell you how happy that will make Felicity."

I didn't say it, but the only person I cared about being happy was Saffron. And that, I wanted with all my heart.

Saffron came into the kitchen a few minutes later and set to work making her grandmother's stuffing. I couldn't keep my eyes off her—the way her brow furrowed in concentration as she chopped celery into uniform-size pieces and how she stuck her tongue out as she measured the turkey stock before adding it.

"What are you thinking about?" Diana asked, appearing at my elbow.

"I'll never tell." I winked.

"You don't need to say anything. You're watching my daughter like she hung the moon."

Heat crept up my neck. "I'm pretty sure she did."

She squeezed my arm. "She deserves someone who looks at her the way you do."

"Not someone. *Me.*"

She laughed. "Better hurry up and do something about it, then. She's been waiting on you forever."

I wanted to tell her that it had been me waiting on Saffron. Since I was old enough to understand what forever meant. But the words stuck in my throat.

She must've seen something in my face because she patted my arm and moved away, leaving me there, peeling more potatoes and thinking about rings and proposals and futures I desperately wanted but was terrified to jinx.

Eventually, the table was set, the food was ready, and we all gathered. Wagner invited Lucas to sit at the head, and once we all took our places, he quietly surveyed his family.

"Before we eat," he said, "I want to say something." His gaze met Diana's, and she dabbed the corners of her eyes with her napkin.

"This has been a hard few months. Worrying about Felicity, about the baby. These last few weeks especially." He stopped for a moment and took a deep breath before continuing. "But sitting here now, seeing all of you, my beautiful granddaughter"—he gestured toward Beatrice in Felicity's arms—"it really shows what's truly important in life."

Diana's hand covered his on the table.

"It isn't a plot of land or a bunch of barrels of wine. It's this. It's family. It's being here for each other." He turned to Diana. "Your mom and I have been talking."

Next to me, Saffron tensed.

"We've been so focused on the winery, on the legacy, on keeping things going the way they've always been. And maybe—" His voice caught, and he cleared his throat. "Maybe it's time to let go of that. To accept that things change. That family matters more than property."

Under the table, I found Saffron's hand and squeezed. Her fingers gripped mine so hard it hurt.

I wondered if she thought he was giving up, surrendering, in the same way it sounded to me. That he was reframing the foreclosure as a choice, as if letting go was somehow noble instead of heartbreaking.

"We can get through anything as long as we have each other. We can face whatever comes. Because we have each other. That's what really matters."

He raised his glass. "To family. To health. To what truly matters."

"To family," everyone echoed, raising their glasses too.

I drank but couldn't taste the wine. Next to me, Saffron barely moved.

Conversation resumed around us—passing dishes, compliments to the chef, normal Thanksgiving chatter. But Saffron picked at the food on her plate.

Lucas, though, appeared lighter. Almost at peace. Maybe the time away, being here with his daughter and son-in-law, waiting for the baby to be born, had given him the time he needed to convince himself that letting the winery go was the right choice.

But what he didn't know was how hard his younger daughter was fighting for him. For their family.

And if she told him now and the wine failed—what would that do to him? To them?

After dinner, after the dishes were done and everyone had retreated to various corners of the house to recover from too much food, I found Saffron outside on the back patio.

She sat on the steps with her arms wrapped around her knees, gazing out at the dark vineyard.

I sat next to her without speaking. The November night was cool, stars were visible above us, and faint sounds of conversation drifted from inside the house.

"He's given up," she murmured.

"I know."

"He's already accepted losing everything."

"I think you're right."

Silence stretched between us.

"I should tell him about the wine."

"Should you?" I asked.

She turned toward me. "I don't know. I mean, he seems at peace. And if I give him hope and things don't go the way I want them to, then what?"

I wanted to assure her that if her dream about the Christmas Blessing Wine didn't turn out the way we both wanted it to, there were other options. Lots of them. Some of which could be handled with a simple phone call. But I didn't. That would be giving up before we had the chance to succeed. And Saffron needed that success. As much for herself as for her family.

Back in the bedroom hours later, we moved around each other, getting ready for bed. The silence was weighted with everything I hadn't said and wondered if I should have. We brushed our teeth, standing next to each other, going through the motions without speaking. In bed, we lay side by side, staring into each other's eyes.

I cupped her cheek. "Saffron, I love—"

She kissed me, stopping me from finishing what I wanted to say, to tell her, more than anything else. I loved her. I was in love with her, and I wanted to spend the rest of my life showing her exactly how much.

I drew her closer, and she came willingly, pressing against me. We made love, slow and quiet, saying with our bodies what she wouldn't let me say with words. Her hands in my hair. Mine tracing her spine. Both of us desperate and gentle and aching.

After, we lay tangled, her head on my chest and my hand in her hair.

It was like we were in a holding pattern. Until we knew that our plan worked, we couldn't move forward with our lives. But we were here, holding each other, and for now, that had to be enough.

Morning arrived gray and subdued. We packed our things in silence.

Downstairs, the family gathered to say goodbye.

Lucas took me aside. "Thanks for coming. It meant a lot to Saffron. To all of us."

"Thanks for having me, sir."

Diana hugged us both. "Drive safe."

Felicity appeared with Beatrice. "See you soon. And, Saff?" She waited until her sister gazed at her. "Tell him."

"I will," she said almost too quietly for me to hear.

We climbed into my truck and left. Four hours back to Paso Robles stretched ahead of us.

The first hour passed mostly in silence. Saffron looked through the window at vineyards rolling past, and I kept my eyes on the road.

"I do, you know."

"Do what?" I asked.

"Feel the same way. About you."

My gut clenched and my heart soared at the same time.

"But I'm scared," she continued. "Terrified, actually. Of needing you this much. Of what happens if—"

"If what?"

"If the wine doesn't work. If I fail anyway." She turned toward me. "I don't know who I am if I'm not the person holding everything together."

"You're the woman I care about more than anyone. That's who you are."

"Is it enough?"

"Absolutely, Saff. It's everything."

We stopped to get gas an hour later, and while I filled the tank, she went inside to get us both coffee. She returned and stood near my truck.

"I'm sorry I didn't let you say it."

"You weren't ready to hear it."

"I want to be. I just—I need to figure who I am. You know?"

I kissed her forehead. "Take all the time you need, sweetheart."

"Because you're not going anywhere?"

I smiled. "Not unless you're with me."

I wished that was enough, but I could tell it wasn't. I rested my head against the seat, thinking about how many people gave me shit about taking long enough to realize Saffron and I were meant to be together. I suppose I had, but what they didn't realize was that it didn't matter whether I was ready for us to commit to each other forever; it was Saffron who wasn't there yet.

16

Saffron

The stack of bills on my desk hadn't shrunk since I'd moved them from the kitchen table to the winery office. Equipment suppliers demanding payment. Distributor notices threatening to suspend our account. Twenty-six days remained until New Year's Eve, and every envelope felt like another nail in a coffin.

My phone rang, and Mom's name lit up the screen.

"Honey, we're coming home tomorrow," she said when I picked up.

I sat up straight, my heart slamming against my ribs. "Tomorrow? Already?"

"Beatrice is growing like a weed and keeping her parents up all night, and the doctor says she's meeting all of her milestones on time or early." My mom's voice softened with emotion. "Felicity and Wagner need this time on their own to figure out how to be a family. And honestly, sweetheart, we miss home. We miss you."

Friday. The wine had been integrating for almost a week, which meant it would be ready to taste on Friday, the same day my parents were coming home.

"That's great, Mom. I can't wait to see you both," I said, hoping I sounded at least a little sincere.

"We should be home in time for dinner. Maybe we can all eat together? I've missed cooking in my own kitchen almost as much as I've missed sleeping in my own bed."

"That sounds perfect. I'll make sure the house is ready."

After we hung up, I stared at my phone for several seconds before pulling up my text thread with Snapper.

My parents coming home tomorrow.

His response came within seconds. *Good timing?*

Or terrible. What if it's not good enough?

Then, we figure out what's wrong and fix it. We still have time.

What if we can't fix it?

Three dots appeared, disappeared, then his message came through. *Come over tonight. I'll make you dinner, and we can worry about tomorrow together. Or I can distract you from worrying. Your choice.*

The tension in my shoulders eased. *Is that your way of saying you're going to seduce me into forgetting my problems?*

It's worked pretty well so far.

I smiled despite the anxiety churning in my stomach. *What's for dinner?*

Whatever you want. I'll even let you have some of my food since you always seem to prefer it over your own.

I do not prefer your food.

Saff, you've been reaching across the table since we were twelve. You're not fooling anyone.

My smile stretched wider. *Fine. But only because you're a better cook than I am.*

I never thought you'd admit it.

Don't let it go to your head.

Too late. See you in an hour?

I'll be there.

I set the phone down and looked around the office at the dusty filing cabinets full of records going back three generations. Faded photos lined the wall behind me, including one of my grandfather standing proudly beside oak barrels, his smile wide and confident in a way I couldn't imagine feeling right now. The window looked out over vines my family had tended for decades, and I let myself wonder if we'd still be tending them come spring.

Tomorrow, everything would change. One way or another.

Snapper's distraction worked exactly as promised. He made pasta with a sauce he'd learned from his mother, poured wine from his family's cellar, and kept up a steady stream of conversation that kept me distracted. We talked about everything except the tasting, everything except foreclosures and deadlines and all the ways this could go wrong.

After dinner, he led me to his bedroom and took his time undressing me, his hands slow and reverent against my skin. He kissed the worry lines between my brows, the tension knots in my shoulders, and the places where I'd been holding stress without even realizing it. When I finally fell asleep in his arms, I didn't dream about losing the winery. I dreamed about him.

I drove home the next morning with my body loose and satisfied and my mind clearer than it had been in days. The memory of his mouth on my neck and his whispered promises in the dark kept me calm while I straightened the house and waited for my parents.

By five o'clock, I was pacing in the kitchen, too anxious to sit still.

When their car turned into the driveway, I was out the door and down the steps before they'd even parked. Dad climbed out first, looking tired but happy, his shoulders more relaxed than I'd seen them in months. Mom followed, already reaching for me with both arms.

"There's my girl." Until she hugged me, I hadn't realized how much I needed it. "God, I missed you so much."

"I missed you too, Mom. Both of you."

Dad wrapped his arms around both of us, and for a moment, we just stood there in the driveway, the three of us together at home for the first time in weeks. The late-afternoon sun was warm on my back, and I let myself sink into the comfort of being held by my parents.

"The place looks good," Dad said when we broke apart. He glanced around the property with the assessing eye of a man who'd spent his entire life working this land. His gaze moved from the bare vines to the winery building and to the house that had been in our family for generations. "Thanks for managing everything while we were gone. I'm proud of you, honey."

Guilt twisted in my chest because I hadn't just been managing the property. I'd been keeping secrets, making plans, betting everything on a whim that might not even work. "Yeah, I've been keeping busy. I had help, though."

My mom's brow arched. "From Snapper?"

Heat flooded my cheeks. "Among others."

My parents exchanged a look that communicated an entire conversation without either of them needing to speak. Dad's mouth twitched like he was fighting a smile, and Mom's eyes sparkled with the kind of curiosity that meant she'd be asking more questions later.

"Let's get your bags inside," I said quickly, desperate to change the subject.

I busied myself carrying their luggage while they walked through the house, reacquainting themselves with home. My mom ran her hand along the kitchen counter like she was greeting an old friend. Dad stood at the window overlooking the vineyard and just breathed for a minute, his shoulders rising and falling with what looked like relief.

I made sandwiches that nobody really ate. We sat around the kitchen table and talked about Beatrice, about Felicity adjusting to motherhood, and Wagner learning to change diapers without gagging. It was a normal conversation that felt anything but because I knew what was coming.

Dad set down his half-eaten sandwich and cleared his throat. "There's something we need to talk about."

I knew what was coming. He was going to say out loud what he'd only alluded to at Thanksgiving. His speech about family mattering more than land or barrels had made it clear he'd already accepted defeat, but he hadn't actually told me the details. Hadn't admitted to his younger daughter that everything was falling apart.

But I couldn't let him say it. Not yet.

"Actually, there's something I need to show you first."

Dad shook his head. "Saffron, honey, please. I need you to listen to me. This is important."

"I know it is, Dad. And I promise I'll listen. But later, okay? Right now, we need to go to Los Caballeros. We need to be there by six."

His brow furrowed with confusion. "Los Caballeros? Why? What's going on?"

"I can't explain it here. You need to see it. Both of you."

My mother reached across the table and put her hand over mine. "Sweetheart, you're shaking. Whatever is going on, you can tell us."

"I know. But this is something I need to show you, not tell you. Please just come with me."

They looked at each other. Then my father said, "Okay. Let's go."

We loaded into my parents' SUV. My dad offered to sit in the back so my mother and I could chat. Not that we did.

My nerves made it impossible to sit still. My knee bounced. My stomach churned. There were too many variables and far too much riding on this single evening.

The drive to Los Cab felt endless even though it only took fifteen minutes. Mom asked questions I deflected. My father's reflection in the rearview mirror looked older than I remembered, even from Thanksgiving, as he watched the vineyards roll past with a troubled expression.

When we drove through the gates and parked near the caves, my hands were shaking badly enough that I had trouble turning off the ignition.

"Saffron. What's going on?"

"You'll know soon. I promise."

"Then, let's go see what has you so wound up."

I led them into the caves and to the main barrel room. Voices echoed ahead of us. Lots of them.

When we rounded the corner, I stopped to take in the scene that Snapper and his family had arranged.

A long table had been set up in the center of the space, glasses were arranged in neat rows, and a barrel mounted on a rack had been tapped. Candles flickered on the ledges carved into the stone walls, casting warm light across the faces of those in the room.

More than thirty people had come together. Snapper's three older brothers were there with their wives as well as Kick, Alex, and Maddox. Tryst stood with a group of my father's closest friends in the world.

I watched his expression shift from confusion to recognition as he took in the scene.

"What's going on?" His words carried an edge of wariness as he approached them. "Why is everyone here?"

"A very special tasting. One we are so happy you're here for," Tryst said, welcoming both my parents with open arms.

One by one, the other men approached with warm expressions, joking and laughing, clapping him on the shoulder and congratulating the family on the birth of their first grandchild.

I'd expected to see pity on their faces. Maybe not all, but a few. Except none looked at my father with anything but happiness to see him. I eavesdropped as they talked about old times, about harvests from decades past, about the way things used to be before "the young guns took over all the wineries." Whatever discomfort Dad had felt seemed to ease as Hewitt Ridge recollected the disastrous crush they'd all experienced years ago.

"We came through that unscathed because we banded together. Remember, guys?" Hewitt said.

Murmurs of agreement came from around the room.

"Hey, beautiful girl," Snapper said. When he put his arm around my shoulders and kissed my temple, everything else faded into background noise. "How are you holding up?"

"Trying to hold it all together."

His hand found the small of my back and stayed there. "I think everyone's here. Ready to start?"

I took a deep breath, squared my shoulders, and addressed the room. "Dad, Mom, I have an announcement to make."

Conversations died away, and everyone turned to face me.

My voice shook when I started speaking. "I was cleaning out the attic while you were in Napa. I know that's probably not surprising since I've never been able to sit still when there's work to be done."

My father's mouth curved into a grin. "That's our Saffron. Always has to be doing something."

A few chuckles rippled through the room, and the warmth and affection in those sounds steadied me enough to continue.

"I found something while I was up there. Marilyn Hope's journal from 1955, the one she kept when she and Concepción Avila made the Christmas Blessing Wine."

Confusion flickered across my parents' faces, but I kept going before they could interrupt with questions.

"I found the journal the day after I overheard your phone call, Dad." I didn't say more than that. While I wanted him to know that I was aware of the impending foreclosure, the last thing I would ever do was humiliate him.

"Finding it gave me an idea," I continued, feeling more confident when Snapper's hand pressed more firmly against my back. "I talked to Snapper about it, and we came up with a plan. The Hopes and Avilas would partner to make this wine together, the way our grandmothers did seventy years ago. Everyone in this room helped make it happen, and the plan is to split the profits between our two families."

My dad's eyes scrunched, and my mother's filled with tears, but before either could speak, I turned to Cru. "Can you take it from here?" I asked.

He cleared his throat and rested his hand on the tapped barrel. "Our original projections were for fifteen hundred bottles, but since we harvested before we had the exact blend percentages figured out, we ended up with more juice than we anticipated. Now, I think we have enough for at least two thousand bottles, maybe more."

My parents looked confused about the reference to percentages, as I filed away the happy surprise of having more wine than we'd originally planned. Snapper's arm came around my shoulders and squeezed gently.

"Our plan is to hold an auction," I said when Cru looked over at me. "Between Christmas and New Year's Eve."

Both my parents understood the significance of that timing. I saw it in the way my mom's hand found Dad's as he struggled to maintain his composure.

His gaze met mine, then he perused the room slowly, meeting the eyes of each person in the room. One by one, they raised their empty glasses in his direction. These were his peers, his friends, people who had worked beside him for decades, and each connected look communicated solidarity.

Tears filled his eyes. His mouth opened, closed, opened again, but nothing came out.

My mom stepped forward and pulled me into a fierce hug, and I realized she was crying.

"My brave girl," she whispered against my hair. "My stubborn, brilliant, wonderful girl. You did all this?"

"Not alone," I said, looking up at Snapper. When she released me, she embraced him equally hard, then took my hand.

"Saffron Hope, you are the most infuriatingly independent person I have ever known. You get it from your father." She laughed through her tears and hugged me again. "I am so proud of you. So incredibly proud."

When she let go, Dad was there. He didn't say anything at first, just wrapped me in a hug that felt like it was holding both of us up, but I could feel him trembling.

"I'm sorry," he said quietly. "I should have told you what was happening. I should have told you the truth instead of trying to protect you from it."

"It's okay, Dad."

"No, it isn't. But we're going to make it okay." He looked at me with red-rimmed eyes. "Thank you, Saffron."

"You're welcome." I gestured toward the barrel before I could talk myself out of it. "Shall we taste?"

Just as Cru moved toward it, I heard him say to Snapper, "What's she doing here?"

I turned to look. *"Isabel?"*

"I heard there was a special tasting taking place tonight. I didn't want to miss it." She glanced around the room until her gaze landed on Kick. "No one minds, right?"

Kick shook his head.

"What in the hell is going on?" Snapper whispered in my ear.

"No idea," I whispered back. "But let's not allow her to ruin this."

"Okay, everyone. Let's get wine in those glasses you're all holding."

Everyone moved toward the barrel and formed a loose line with my parents in front. Cru poured a couple of ounces for everyone until he reached the end of the line, where Snapper and I stood.

"We're tasting this for the first time together," he said, raising his glass to us, then facing those in the room. "Everyone here had a hand in creating what's in this wine that represents more than just the Hopes and the Avilas. It represents the collection of families who were the founders of the Central Coast wine region. The blend we're about to sample is forty percent Gamay, thirty-five percent Syrah, and twenty-five percent Zinfandel. We used whole-cluster carbonic maceration, then pressed and completed the alcoholic fermentation in stainless tanks. The three-varietal blend has been integrating for eight days." Cru raised his glass in the air once more. "May Bacchus grant his favor on the Christmas Blessing Wine."

"Hear, hear," Snapper and I said simultaneously as we took our places around the long table.

After taking a deep breath, I held my glass up to the light and examined what we'd created. The color was a beautiful, deep ruby with hints of garnet at the edge.

"Excellent color development," Tryst commented, and I agreed. It was remarkable, given how young the wine was.

The second step was swirling and sniffing. I brought the glass to my nose and inhaled deeply, letting the aromatics fill my senses. Complex layers were immediately apparent—also extraordinary. Dark fruit—blackberry, black cherry, and hints of plum—dominated, followed by clove, black pepper, and cinnamon. Underneath it all were rich earths like forest floor and turned soil after rain.

"Nice nose," Bit said from where he and Eberly stood across from us.

The third step was tasting. This was the moment everything came down to.

I raised the glass to my lips and let the wine flow over my tongue.

My first impression was that the wine was good. Really good, actually.

The fruit came forward immediately but was balanced by the structure underneath. The tannins had integrated beautifully, smooth rather than harsh or grippy. I could taste the backbone of the wine, the architecture that would let it age well. The acidity was bright and clean, lifting the fruit and keeping everything fresh.

I swallowed and tasted again, searching for that transcendent quality, the spark that made people remember a wine seventy years after they'd tasted it—something extraordinary to bloom across my tongue, for the kind of experience that would make collectors fight over the right to own a bottle.

But it wasn't there.

The wine was good. The kind of wine any winemaker would be proud to produce. Well-made. Balanced. Drinkable. Something I could serve at any dinner table without a moment's hesitation.

But not extraordinary. Not the kind of wine that would command auction prices high enough to save us.

I looked around the table at the faces of the people who had helped create this. Everyone was tasting with the focus and concentration of experienced winemakers doing what they did best. They swirled their glasses, tasted again, held the wine in their mouths before swallowing, evaluated, and considered with decades of combined experience.

A long silence stretched out across the room. Nobody wanted to speak first.

Finally, Brix broke the quiet. "This is really well-made wine." His comment was measured and thoughtful but conveyed more in what he didn't say.

"Beautiful balance," Noah Ridge added.

"It's definitely market-worthy," said Kick.

All of those assessments were accurate. All of them were complimentary. And all of them were devastating.

Because it wasn't enough. We needed something that would make wealthy collectors open their wallets wide enough to save us from foreclosure.

"It's lovely," Tryst said with the kind of sympathy that made my stomach drop. "Truly."

A pause stretched out.

"But something's missing," I said, forcing myself to say what we all knew. "Isn't it?"

Everyone in the room seemed to exhale at once, relieved that someone had said what we all were thinking.

Martin Barrett spoke up first. "Something is definitely missing. I can taste the absence of it, but I can't define what it is."

"It needs depth. Or weight. Some kind of bridge between the fresh fruit and something more substantial underneath," Hewitt suggested.

"Like it's missing a foundation," Brix added. "Or maybe a top note. There's a component that should be there to complete the blend, but I can't identify what it would be."

Discussion swirled around me as those who'd tasted tried to puzzle out what was wrong. They talked about pH levels and acid balance and tannin structure. They debated whether the issue was with one of the varietals or with the blend ratios or with the fermentation process. All the measurements had been perfect, they agreed, but somehow, the wine was still incomplete.

I couldn't hear most of it over my pulse roaring in my ears.

I had failed. I looked at my father across the table.

Dad was tasting and retasting, evaluating honestly with decades of experience behind it. He knew wine better than almost anyone I'd ever met, and I could see him searching for the same thing I'd been looking for. That spark. That magic. When his eyes met mine, I saw everything in his expression. Pride in what I had attempted. Sorrow that it wasn't enough. Gratitude for the friends who had helped us. And heartbreak, deep and raw, because this beautiful wine wasn't going to save us after all.

My mom's hand rested on his arm. Both of them understood what this meant. Their daughter had made beautiful wine with the best help she could find. But beautiful wasn't going to be enough.

Snapper's arm went around my shoulders, and I rested against him because I needed his warmth and his steadiness. He didn't offer empty reassurances or hollow promises that everything would be fine. He just held me while I stared into my glass of disappointment.

"We still have time," said Cru. "We'll figure it out."

But looking at the faces around me, at the people who'd spent their entire lives crafting wine, none of them seemed to know how to fix it.

The expression on one person's face, though, chilled me to the bone. Isabel Van Orr looked *triumphant*. Like this was somehow a competition between just the two of us and she'd just won.

"Where is everyone?" I heard someone say from the cave's outer corridor.

"Baron!" said Tryst. "Welcome back. When did you get in?"

He stepped into the room, looking around with curiosity, especially when he noticed his daughter's presence.

"I flew in for Thanksgiving, and when I saw the notice about tonight's meeting, I came straight here."

While Baron took in the gathering with growing interest, every time he looked in Isabel's direction, his brow furrowed.

"So what is all this?" he asked, motioning to the table with its rows of glasses, then to the tapped barrel. "Are we tasting a special vintage? May I join you?"

"Of course," said Cru, pouring a glass and handing it over without comment.

Like we all had, Baron held the wine up to the light to examine the color, then he swirled, bringing it to his nose and breathing deeply. His eyes closed as he concentrated on the aromatics. Collectively, we went still as he took a sip and held the wine in his mouth for several seconds before swallowing.

Then, he set his glass down on the table. His gaze connected with Tryst's, then my father's, then mine.

"This is the Christmas Blessing Wine." It wasn't a question. It was a statement of fact from a man who knew exactly what he was tasting.

He was met with stunned silence. Nobody had expected Baron Van Orr to walk in and immediately identify what we'd been trying to create.

"Something is missing." His said with absolute certainty. "And I know exactly what it is."

17

Snapper

Baron Van Orr set his wineglass on the table. The barrel room had gone quiet enough that I heard the clink of glass against wood.

"I know exactly what's missing." He raised his glass again and held it to the light a second time. "It's missing the Van Orr blend—my grandmother's contribution."

Saffron's head shot up. "By any chance, was her name Ellen?"

Baron's eyes widened. "Yes, it was. What makes you ask?"

"We found a photo of her with my great-grandmother, Marilyn, and Concepción Avila. No one could identify her," Saffron explained.

"Then we found an entry in Concepción's journal that was written in February, two months after the first Christmas Blessing Wine was released. It said, 'E says she won't allow us to make the wine again.' Do you know why?" I asked.

"Sadly, I do." Baron took a seat at the table. "Your great-grandmothers were the winemakers. They came up with the original formula, and their two families worked together to create the wine. However, when they first tasted it, they knew something was missing."

"Just like this," I said, raising my own glass.

"My grandmother was good friends with the two women and suggested what became the final component—an aged blend from the Van Orr family cellars. As far as why the wine was never made again, I didn't know the full story until I was sixteen," Baron continued. "My father sat me down, opened one of the last remaining bottles, and told me everything. He said he was doing it to teach me a lesson. About pride. About ego. About the cost of both."

No one in the room spoke.

"My grandmother made a choice that my father said brought a great deal of shame to our family."

"What choice?" Tryst asked.

"To let her pride destroy something beautiful."

Baron took a breath, and my hand found Saffron's under the table.

"Marilyn and Concepción's original idea was to raise money for those struggling during the holidays.

That year had been particularly hard on many families in the valley. Bad weather, poor harvests, economic struggles." Baron looked between Saffron and me. "Your great-grandmothers were brilliant. Winemakers ahead of their time."

Then his gaze shifted to Tryst. "You remember."

Tryst's eyes shone and he smiled. "I do."

"They developed the formula using their combined expertise," Baron continued. "California and Spanish ancestral techniques. The carbonic maceration was revolutionary for the time. My grandmother didn't create anything. She provided access to something that already existed.

"Her father—my great-grandfather—had bottled a particular vintage for family only. By all accounts, it was extraordinary, but the production was limited. Ellen suggested they try blending a little with the wine they'd made. It wasn't much, maybe ten percent of the total volume. But it was the missing piece. The bridge between young fruit and aged complexity."

Exactly what our wine was missing.

"The limited run sold out in hours and raised enough money that local families were able to have a nice Christmas. It saved many of them from losing everything." He paused. "Then a prominent industry publication wrote about the charitable project and praised the wine's quality."

My chest tightened when I realized where the story was going.

"The article gave Marilyn and Concepción all the credit, as was only right. My grandmother's name was never mentioned."

"That's why she was unwilling to give them what they needed to make it again," I said. "But why didn't your great-grandfather intervene?"

"Both he and my grandfather, Ellen's husband, were deceased by then, and it was her decision alone." He shook his head. "She lost so much because of it, including two of her closest friends." Baron removed his glasses and scrubbed his face with his hand. "On her deathbed, she told my dad the story and how she regretted that decision her entire life."

I glanced over at Isabel, who stood near the back of the room with her arms crossed. She was too far away for me to know for certain, but it appeared she might be crying.

Tryst stepped forward. "Baron, do any of those bottles still exist?"

"A few. My father kept them in our private cellar."
Baron set down his wineglass.

Hope flickered in my chest, and I felt Saffron tense
beside me.

"Can we go look?" I asked.

"Of course. Who is coming?" Baron asked.

"Saffron and me for now," I said, taking her hand.

"We'll come too," said Kick, who was following
behind us with Isabel.

While I wanted to say no, it wasn't really my call.
We were headed to her family's cellars.

The drive to the Van Orr estate only took a few minutes. We parked near the winery and followed Baron
inside. He led us deep into the cellar, to a room in the
very back. We waited while he sorted through several
keys before finding the right one. The lock clicked, and
the door swung open with a groan that echoed off the
stone walls.

Inside, the space was small—maybe twenty by
twenty—lined with wooden racks that held bottles
covered in decades of dust. Baron moved along the
racks methodically, his finger tracing along labels,
searching. His movements grew more agitated as he
checked each rack. Once. Twice. A third time.

"They should be here." His voice was tight. "Right here, in this section."

He moved bottles, checked behind them, and did the same at the next rack.

"They're gone." His face pale and his breathing heavy. "The bottles are gone."

My stomach dropped.

Baron's gaze swept across those of us in the space, then locked on his daughter.

A weighted look passed between them.

"Isabel, do you know what happened to the bottles?"

We all turned toward her.

Her composure, which had been so carefully maintained all evening, cracked. Her chin trembled, and tears filled her eyes.

"I—" She pressed her hands to her face.

Kick, who was standing beside her, whispered something in her ear I couldn't hear.

She shook her head, unable or unwilling to speak.

"Isabel?" Do you have something to say?" Baron asked.

"You don't understand." Her words came out choked. "None of you understand what it's like."

"What what's like?" I asked.

She glanced at Kick, then at me. "I know about your little arrangement. How the two of you conspired against me, not just this year but in the past."

"What are you talking about?" Baron asked.

"For the last five years, Snapper paid to have Saffron bid against me at the bachelor auction just so I wouldn't win. That's how much he didn't want to take me on a stupid date. And this year, he was willing to put up seventy-five grand just to avoid what? Having to sit across a table from me and have dinner?" Her eyes filled with tears again that she tried to wipe away, but they fell too fast. "Am I really that bad?"

I took a step in her direction, and Kick shifted so he was between her and me.

"What the hell?" I said, glaring at him.

"You—"

Isabel interrupted him. "I don't need you to stick up for me, Rascon. For all I know, you told me on purpose."

When my brother's face turned ten shades of red, I knew she was telling the truth. While I wanted to throat punch him, now wasn't the time. Later? Absolutely.

"He also told me that, in exchange for saving you from having to take me on a date, Saffron asked you to help her make the Christmas Blessing Wine."

I clenched my fists at my sides and was moving in my brother's direction when Saffron put her hand on my arm.

"Don't," she whispered. "Let her finish."

"Do you know what people say about me?" Isabel's tone sharpened. "That I'm desperate. Pathetic. Last year, someone made a betting pool on social media about how much I'd bid—" She stopped. "But I suppose you both knew that already."

Guilt hit me like a fist to the gut.

She turned to her father. "I found Grandmother Ellen's journal after Mom died. I was snooping in your study. The whole story was there. What she contributed to the wine. Then I went looking for the bottles that remained and found them in here."

Baron's expression was unreadable.

"When Kick told me what they'd been doing, I immediately knew what you'd need to finish it."

"Is that why you came tonight? To rub our noses in it? Do you even know why Saffron wanted to make the wine? What's at stake?"

"You're right about why I showed up at Los Cab."

"Isabel," Baron said carefully. "Where is the wine?"

"The night Kick told me the truth about the auction, I was so angry, so hurt, I came here, intending to smash every single bottle. To destroy any chance you'd have to finish the wine."

The room went dead quiet.

Saffron stood perfectly still beside me, her arms wrapped around herself.

"You said you intended to smash every bottle," I said quietly, watching Isabel's face. "What did you do instead?"

Isabel's expression shifted. "I didn't do it." She looked at her father. "Then tonight, when I heard you tell the story about why Ellen wouldn't give them the wine—" Her voice cracked. "About her regret…"

"Where is the wine?" Baron repeated.

"I'll show you—"

"Wait," said Saffron. She'd straightened and dropped her arms to her sides, but her face was deathly pale.

When I reached for her hand, she turned to Isabel. "You're right. What we did was wrong."

"This isn't on you, Saffron. It was me—" I started.

"No, it wasn't just you, Snapper. I could've said no." Her eyes scrunched, then filled with tears. "I'm sorry, Isabel. For all of it. For making you feel that way. It was cruel, and I'm—I'm so sorry."

Isabel stared at her, as if the apology stunned her.

"It's over. We're not releasing the wine," Saffron continued. "Not like this. Not when it's built on hurting someone."

"What?" The word came out sharper than I intended. "Saffron, you can't just give up—"

"Some things matter more than the winery. My father knows it, and so do I." She stepped closer to Isabel. "The cycle of hurt ends here. Tonight."

"That's the stupidest thing I've ever heard," Isabel said flatly.

Saffron blinked. "What?"

"You don't get to give up and call it noble." Isabel squared her shoulders. "That's not ending the cycle. That's just quitting."

"I don't understand—"

Isabel stepped closer too. "I'm not letting you give up." Isabel looked between us. "You, me, and Snapper are going to finish what our grandmothers started. That's how this ends. Not with you martyring your-self. Yes, the cycle of hurt ends now, but not because we quit."

Saffron opened her mouth, then closed it.

"I heard everything my father said tonight. Ellen let pride destroy something beautiful," Isabel continued. "I'm not making that mistake. I'm not living a life of regret like she did. And I'm not going to let you either." She held out her hand. "Partners?"

Saffron stared at Isabel's outstretched hand for several seconds, then closed the distance between them and hugged her instead. "Partners," I heard her say.

18

Saffron

The December morning was cold enough that I could see my breath as Snapper and I walked into the Los Caballeros winery production area. The fermentation tanks stood in neat rows, their stainless-steel surfaces beaded with condensation. Our wine—the Christmas Blessing Wine—rested inside three of them, waiting.

Baron Van Orr stood near the tasting table with three wooden cases stacked beside him. He looked older than I remembered, his face lined with exhaustion or emotion or both.

"These are the last of the Van Orr Family Private Reserve," he said, resting his hand on the top case. "What my grandmother contributed to the original blend."

My father moved closer to examine the bottles Baron was pulling from the first case. The labels were hand-written in faded ink, and I counted twelve bottles per case. Thirty-six bottles in total.

"Do you know the amount used?" Cru asked.

"Ten percent of total volume." Baron's hands trembled as he set bottles on the table. "Two hundred liters."

I watched him line up the bottles like soldiers preparing for battle. Each one represented a piece of his family's history, his grandmother's pride, decades of regret being put to rest.

Movement near the doorway caught my attention. Kick had arrived, standing just inside the entrance like he wasn't sure he belonged here. Snapper's entire body went rigid beside me. His jaw clenched, and I heard him exhale through his nose—the kind of controlled breathing people did when they were trying not to explode.

The conversation from last night came flooding back. Snapper pacing at his house at midnight, too angry to sleep. "I've never been this angry with him."

Kick had betrayed his confidence twice. And to Isabel, which made it so much worse. Nobody seemed to know for certain whether the two were involved, and asking felt like stepping into a minefield.

"Let's get started," Cru said, pulling my attention back to the wine.

Baron opened the first bottle with reverence, then continued in the same manner, handing them down the line. We measured and poured, transferring the precious liquid into larger vessels. Baron opened bottle after bottle, the aged wine pooling together until we had enough to blend into our tanks. My mother stood beside my father, both of them watching with expressions I couldn't quite read. Hope mixed with fear mixed with wonder.

Cru opened the valve on the first tank, and we watched the Van Orr Private Reserve disappear into our creation. The wine swirled together, young meeting old, three families reuniting after seventy years of separation.

"Thirty minutes for initial integration," Cru announced. "Then we taste."

Those thirty minutes crawled by. I paced between the tanks and the tasting table until Snapper caught my hand and pulled me against his side. His warmth steadied me, but I could feel the tension radiating through his body. He kept glancing at Kick, who stood on the opposite side of the room, examining equipment he probably knew better than his own reflection.

Isabel arrived halfway through the wait, but she and Kick didn't speak or even acknowledge one another's presence. Curious as I was, it was none of my business.

"It's time," Cru said, drawing samples from each tank, filling the glasses that he distributed around the table. I held mine up to the light. The color looked the same—deep ruby with garnet edges—but when I brought it to my nose, everything had changed.

The bright fruit was still there, but now, it had a foundation. The aged wine had given our young blend something to stand on. Berry and plum and cherry layered over earth and leather and time itself.

I tasted.

The wine hit my tongue, and I understood immediately what had been missing. The Van Orr component bridged the gap between fresh and complex, between promising and complete. The tannins that had been good were now remarkable. The acidity that had been balanced now sang. The finish went on and on, evolving as I held the wine in my mouth.

"Oh my God," my mother whispered.

Around the table, faces transformed. My father's eyes went wide. Baron pressed his hand to his chest. Even Snapper, who'd been so certain this would work, looked stunned.

"This is it," Snapper said. "This is what they made."

Baron set down his glass with a hand that shook. "My grandmother regretted her choice every single day for the rest of her life. And now—" It was as though his words stuck in his throat.

My father moved around the table, and he and Baron embraced while the wine their grandmothers had created came together again after seven decades apart.

Tears spilled down my cheeks, and I didn't bother wiping them away.

"How long until we can bottle?" I asked.

"Two to four weeks for full integration," Cru said. "The components need time to marry."

Four weeks would put us past New Year's Eve. Past the deadline. Too late to save anything.

"Two weeks, then," I said. "We taste again in two weeks."

"December twenty-third," my father calculated. "If it's ready, we bottle Christmas Eve."

"That gives us one week to get everything to auction," Baron added. "New Year's Eve."

The math was tight. Terrifyingly tight. But it was possible.

"Two weeks," Cru agreed. "December twenty-third."

For the next fourteen days, I existed in a strange suspended state where time moved both agonizingly slowly and impossibly fast.

Snapper and I fell into a routine that should have felt comfortable—sleeping at his place most nights. We'd make love, then he'd pull me against his chest and I'd fall asleep listening to his heartbeat. Every morning, he sneaked out of bed and returned with a cup of coffee for each of us.

But underneath everything ran a current of anxiety I couldn't shake. I couldn't plan. Couldn't think past December twenty-third. Every time someone mentioned Christmas or New Year's or anything beyond the next few days, my mind went blank.

"What do you want for Christmas?" Snapper asked one morning. We were in his kitchen, and I was stealing bacon from his plate even though I'd insisted I wasn't hungry.

"I don't know."

"You don't know, or you can't think about it?"

"Both." I reached for another piece of bacon, and he caught my wrist and brought the piece to his mouth instead. Then he licked my fingers, first making me giggle, then spreading the heat of desire throughout my body. We ended up leaving the rest of the food on the table, uneaten, and returned to the bedroom, where I forgot about everything except the feel of his mouth on mine and the way his hands moved up my spine.

We checked the wine every few days, drawing samples to monitor the integration. Each time, it tasted better. More cohesive. More complete. But would it be ready in time?

"Stop worrying," Snapper said time and again, catching me staring into my glass like I could divine the future from wine.

"I can't help it."

"I know." He took the glass from my hand and set it aside, then put his arms around me. "But worrying won't make it integrate faster."

"As if logic can stop it."

"Fair point."

Lucia would come by the winery whenever she saw Snapper's vehicle parked in front. She never arrived empty-handed, insisting neither her son nor I were eating enough.

"We would love to have you and your family join us for Christmas dinner," she said on one such day. "It would mean so much to have both families together this year."

I told her I'd mention it to my parents, but the weight of the unknown pressed down on my chest. So much rode on the wine currently resting in stainless-steel tanks, counting down to either salvation or devastation. Until I knew which it was, I couldn't think beyond Christmas Eve eve.

Snapper still hadn't spoken to Kick. I noticed it in the way he'd tense whenever his brother's name came up, the way he'd change the subject or suddenly remember something he needed to do in another room.

"You need to talk to him," I said one night. We were lying in his bed, and I could feel the tension radiating through his body despite the late hour.

"I'm not ready."

"When will you be?"

"I don't know." He ran his hand through his hair, making it stand up in ways that would have been funny if the conversation wasn't so serious. "Maybe never."

His evident pain made my chest ache. These were brothers who'd been best friends, roping partners, who'd spent their entire lives joined at the hip. And now, they couldn't occupy the same room.

"He betrayed me, Saff. Twice. How do I get past that?"

I didn't know, so I just held him tighter and hoped it was enough.

December twenty-third arrived cold and clear. I woke in Snapper's bed with my stomach in knots, too nervous to eat the breakfast he'd made. We drove to Los Caballeros in silence, his hand gripping mine so tightly my fingers went numb.

Baron was already there when we arrived at the winery. My parents walked in shortly after us, then Cru appeared from the fermentation room with Isabel at his side. She'd been around more in the past two weeks, and each time, her presence became more comfortable.

"Before we taste," Baron said, reaching into a bag at his feet, "I brought something."

He set two bottles that made my heart stutter on the table. The labels were faded but unmistakable—Christmas Blessing Wine, 1955.

"I thought they were all gone," my father said, barely above a whisper.

"I kept two bottles hidden even deeper than the others." Baron's hands trembled as he reached for them. "I was saving them for—I don't know what. But it seems right to have them now. When the new wine is ready, we can taste them side by side and know if we've honored what our grandmothers created."

The ritual felt ceremonial when Cru drew samples from the tanks—the measured pour, the glass catching light, the moment before tasting when anything was possible or impossible in equal measure.

I raised the glass to my lips and sipped. My eyes nearly rolled back in my head. The wine was transcendent. Every component had integrated completely. The bright fruit of the young wine, the complexity of the aged blend, the structure that came from both—it all worked together in a way that was greater than the sum of its parts. The flavors evolved on my tongue, revealing new layers with each second. Berry and earth and spice and time.

I looked up and saw tears in both my father's eyes and Baron's.

"It's magnificent," my dad whispered.

Baron's hands shook as he raised his glass higher. "To Marilyn, Concepción, and Ellen. May their legacy live on year after year in the wine they were responsible for creating."

My mother pulled me into a fierce hug. Snapper's arm came around both of us. Around the table, everyone tasted again and again, confirming what we all knew. We'd done it. Against all odds, with time running out, we'd actually done it.

"We bottle tomorrow," Cru said. "Christmas Eve."

"I've confirmed the auction is set for New Year's Eve," Baron added. "Press releases went out yesterday. My PR firm is already fielding calls from collectors. The interest is"—he paused, searching for the right word—"extraordinary."

Hope bloomed in my chest so fierce it hurt. We were going to make it. We were actually going to save the winery.

Isabel caught my eye across the table. I moved around to where she stood, and she met me halfway.

"I'll never forget this," I said. "What you did. Insisting we finish the wine instead of letting me give up. I'm so grateful."

"I needed to make amends," she whispered. "For so many things."

"Bygones?"

"Bygones," she agreed, and for the first time in as long as I could remember, her smile looked genuine.

There was frost on the ground Christmas Eve morning when we arrived at Los Caballeros in the predawn darkness. Neither of us had spoken much last night or on our way this morning. It was as though we were both holding our breath, praying yesterday hadn't been a dream.

The bottling facility was already buzzing with activity when we arrived. My parents were there, along with the men who'd agreed to help from the very beginning, when we were out in the vineyards, handpicking. But someone was missing. Kick.

I noticed his absence immediately. Snapper did too—I saw the way his jaw clenched, the way his shoulders went rigid as he scanned the room, looking for his brother. As time went on, I think we both realized he wasn't coming, but neither of us wanted to say it out loud.

Isabel was missing too, which surprised me even more.

The work continued for several hours. Bottles moved down the line, wine flowed from tanks through tubes and filters into glass, then corks were inserted with pneumatic precision. At the end of the line, my mother, Lucia, Daphne, Eberly, and I applied labels, then loaded the bottles into the cases.

The physical labor felt good. Repetitive motion that didn't require thinking. Just doing. Moving through the steps that would result in two thousand bottles of wine I now knew represented so much more than saving our winery.

Hours passed. My back ached. My hands cramped. But we kept going.

Snapper joined us at the labeling station once the bottles were all corked. I told him to take a break, but he said he couldn't. I understood. For me, part of it was that, if I stopped moving, exhaustion would overwhelm me. For him, I wondered if keeping busy helped stop him from thinking about his brother who should have been here and wasn't.

"You okay?" I asked when he came to stand beside me.

"Fine."

"You keep checking your phone. Any news?"

His jaw clenched harder. "None."

"Maybe he doesn't think he's welcome."

"Maybe he's not, and you know what? I don't fucking care."

Tryst appeared beside us with the quiet presence of someone who'd been watching and waiting for the right moment. "May I speak with you both?"

Snapper's shoulders tensed, but he nodded.

"Don't pass judgment before you understand the full story," Tryst said. "Talk to your brother. Listen to what he has to say."

"He lied to me—"

"And you've never made a mistake? Never done something you regretted?" Tryst rested his hand on Snapper's shoulder. "It's Christmas Eve. A time for forgiveness. For family. Heed the lesson from the Christmas Blessing, and do not let pride destroy you."

While Snapper didn't answer, I saw something shift in his expression. Resistance giving way to consideration, even if he wasn't ready to admit it.

When every bottle was labeled and loaded into cases, Baron asked for everyone's attention. "I've just spoken to my contact at the auction house. We're confirmed for seven PM on New Year's Eve. They're expecting record attendance with collectors coming in from around the world."

I closed my eyes and said my own silent prayer of thanks to Marilyn, my great-grandmother, who I was convinced had somehow led me to her journals and gave me the strength to do this.

Snapper and I arrived at my parents' house just as the sun was setting.

"Who's here?" I asked, pointing to an SUV I didn't recognize.

My mother smiled. "You'll see."

We walked inside, and I heard it immediately—a baby crying. Not just any baby.

"Beatrice?" I called out.

"In here!" Felicity shouted from the living room.

I rushed through the house and found my sister on the couch, my niece in her arms, and Wagner standing behind them.

"Oh my God, I'm so happy to see you!" With the baby between us, Felicity and I hugged in the most awkward way possible. "When did you get in?"

"A few hours ago. We wanted to surprise you for Christmas." She looked down at Beatrice, who'd stopped crying and was now staring up at me with dark, unfocused eyes. "She's doing so well. The doctors said her recovery is ahead of schedule."

Relief flooded through me so fiercely it stole my breath. My niece was okay. My sister was here. My parents were home. Snapper stood in the doorway, watching with so much warmth, I was back to fearing I was dreaming.

After a few minutes of listening to stories about my niece's brilliance, I asked Felicity if she'd mind if I took a quick shower.

She waved her hand in front of her face. "If you didn't say you were going to soon, I would've suggested it."

I laughed and shook my head. Some things never change. Like older sisters.

I kissed Snapper's cheek, promising to hurry back as I made my way upstairs. I showered quickly, standing under the hot water just long enough for some of the knots in my shoulders to ease. I changed into clean clothes, ran a comb through my wet hair, and was almost to the bottom of the stairs when I heard Snapper and Felicity speaking quietly in the dining room.

"I need to tell her the truth," Snapper said.

I froze.

"No. It doesn't matter now. Everything worked out. There's no reason she ever needs to know."

"But what if she finds out some other way?"

"How? Who would tell her?"

"I guess you're right. I just feel like I've been lying by omission this whole time."

Lying by omission? The whole time? I covered my mouth with my hand when I felt bile rising in my throat. Everything Isabel had said about Felicity and Snapper came flooding back. About how there had been something between them. Something I didn't know about. Something they'd been hiding.

The walls seemed to close in on me, and my heart hammered against my ribs. All those doubts I'd pushed away, all those fears I'd told myself were baseless, came crashing back with brutal clarity.

While I'd been falling in love with him, while I'd put all my trust in him, he'd been lying. While he'd been angry at his brother for betraying his confidence—he'd been keeping secrets of his own.

With my sister.

I came the rest of the way down the stairs and rounded the corner to the dining room. Felicity and

Snapper were the only two there. Standing too close together, looking guilty as hell.

"So you're angry with Kick for betraying you by not being honest," I said, shaking so hard I could barely speak. "Yet you've been hiding things from me all along. You're not being honest with me either."

Snapper's face lost its color. "Saff—"

"Don't." I held up my hand. "Just don't."

He moved toward me, and I backed away.

"I want you to leave," I said. "Now."

"Please, let me explain—"

"Leave!"

He stood still for several seconds, his expression devastated, his hands reaching for me even though I'd made it clear I didn't want to be touched. Then he turned and walked to the front door. It closed behind him with a soft click that somehow sounded louder than if he'd slammed it.

I looked at my sister, who stood speechless.

I turned and ran upstairs, reached my bedroom, and slammed the door hard enough to rattle the frame. Then I sank onto my bed and let myself fall apart.

19

Snapper

The drive to Los Caballeros felt like it took hours even though it was only twenty minutes. My jaw was clenched so hard it ached. The headlights cut through the darkness, illuminating bare vines that blurred past my windows.

I'd lost her.

The thought kept circling through my head like a vulture waiting for something to die. Maybe it already had. Maybe what Saffron and I had built over the past two months was already gone, killed by secrets I'd kept, thinking I was protecting her.

The main house glowed with lights when I drove through the gates. Cars lined the driveway. My brothers and their families had already arrived for Christmas Eve. Through the windows, I could see movement, and when I got out of my truck, I could hear the faint sound of children's laughter. The kids were probably wound up on sugar and excitement, counting down the hours until morning when they could tear into presents.

I stood in the darkness for several minutes before going inside. My chest felt hollow. My throat burned. How could I join my family and act like everything was fine? How could I paste on a smile and be Uncle Snapper, who let the kids climb all over him, while everyone celebrated?

The front door opened, and Bit appeared on the porch. He was backlit by the warm glow spilling from inside, and after standing still for a few seconds, he started down the steps toward my truck.

"What are you doing here?" he asked. "I thought you were with Saffron."

I opened my mouth to explain, but nothing came out.

"Snap?" He moved closer, and his expression shifted from curious to alarmed. "What happened?"

"It's over."

"Wait. What? Why—" He stopped. "Come on. Let's walk."

I shook my head. "I can't. The kids—"

"The kids are fine. Ma's got them making cookies." He gripped my shoulder. "You need to talk, and you can't do it in there."

The front door opened again, and Tryst stepped out. He took one look at me, then descended the steps with the quiet authority he'd carried my entire life. After my father died, Tryst had stepped in without hesitation. He'd been the one who taught me how to rope, how to handle a stubborn horse, how to be a man when I was just a kid who'd lost his dad.

"Walk with us, Salazar."

Our breath clouded in the cold air, and frost crunched under our boots. Above us, the cloudless sky was bright with stars. The three of us walked a few feet from the house, then Tryst stopped and turned to face me.

"Tell us what happened."

Everything poured out. How I'd gone to the Hopes' house earlier, how happy Saffron had been to see Felicity and the baby, how we'd all been celebrating the wine being bottled. Then, how I'd taken Felicity aside while Saffron was upstairs.

"We were talking in the dining room," I continued. "I was trying to decide whether to tell Saffron something. Felicity said I shouldn't. That it would only hurt her." The memory made my chest tighten. "Saffron came downstairs and overheard us. She heard me say I'd been lying by omission the whole time."

"What were you discussing?" Tryst asked.

"That's what I'm trying to tell you." I took a breath and looked at Bit. "Right after Saffron came to me, asking for help with the wine, you told me you'd heard rumors about Hope Family Winery facing foreclosure."

"I remember."

"Saffron hadn't told me yet. She wouldn't admit anything was wrong. But I knew something was eating at her. I knew she was desperate even if she couldn't bring herself to say why." I shoved my hands in my pockets because they wouldn't stop shaking. "So I went to the bank."

Tryst's expression didn't change, but I saw understanding start to dawn in his eyes.

"I talked to Isaac Brennan. I told him I wanted to know the situation with the Hope account." My confession came faster now, like lancing a wound. "He couldn't give me specifics because of privacy laws, but I told him that whatever shortfall existed, I'd cover it. All of it. Whatever they needed. There was no way in hell I was going to let their family lose everything."

Silence stretched between us. Coyote howled somewhere in the hills.

"You guaranteed their debt," Tryst phrased it as a statement, not a question.

"Exactly."

"Wow," Bit muttered under his breath.

"Did you try to explain?" Tryst asked.

My throat tightened. "She wouldn't let me. She just told me to leave."

"So she doesn't know about the bank," Bit said.

"No. And I don't even know what she thinks I was lying about."

"It isn't what it's about, Salazar. It's the deceit that hurts her," Tryst said quietly.

"I know." I looked down at the ground because I couldn't meet their eyes anymore. "I know it was wrong. I should have told her. But she was so scared, and I just wanted her to have a safety net."

"Your heart was in the right place," Tryst said.

"Was it?" The question came out sharp, angry. Not at him. At myself. "Because I've spent the last two weeks furious with Kick for keeping secrets from me. For lying by omission. For betraying my trust." I looked up. "And I've been doing the exact same thing to Saffron this entire time."

The parallel had been eating at me since the moment Saffron accused me of it.

Bit moved closer and rested his hand on my shoulder. "There is a difference, Snap. Kick betrayed a confidence he swore to keep. You made a financial arrangement to protect the woman you love."

"Does the motivation matter if the result is the same?"

Tryst sighed and looked up at the sky. When he spoke, what he had to say carried the weight of experience, of decades of watching people make mistakes and helping them find their way through. "The motivation matters. But so does the dishonesty. You should have told her."

"I know."

"She would have fought you," Bit added. "Refused to let you do it. Her pride—"

"Her pride is part of what I love about her." I stared out at the dark vineyard. "She's stubborn and independent, and she'd rather break than bend. But that's also why she needed someone to have her back without her knowing. Lucas would never have accepted help either."

"So you were protecting both of them," Tryst said.

"Fat lot of good it did." I sounded bitter because I was. "Now, I've lost her."

"Give her time," Bit said. "Let her cool down. Then see if she'll let you explain."

Tryst studied me. "What else is on your mind, nephew?"

"I need to talk to Kick. It's Christmas, and I've been so angry with him that he's probably sitting somewhere alone, thinking his family doesn't want him around."

Tryst and Bit exchanged glances.

"What?" Dread pooled in my stomach.

"His phone's off," said Bit.

"What do you mean? Since when?"

"Yesterday, then we tried to reach him when he missed the bottling, but we haven't heard anything from him."

The front door of the main house opened, and Ma appeared, silhouetted against the light. She stood there for a moment before stepping onto the porch, wrapping her cardigan tighter around herself.

"Tryst? Trevino?" Her said across the distance. "Is everything all right?"

We walked back toward the house, and Ma's eyes found mine immediately. Even in the dim light from the porch, I could see the worry etched on her face.

"Salazar, you're here. Have you heard from your brother?" she asked before I could say anything.

I didn't need to ask which one. "I haven't, Ma."

"Where is he? Tomorrow is Christmas." Her eyes filled with tears, and I felt like the world's biggest asshole for being angry with my brother instead of making things right before now.

Tryst wrapped his arm around Ma's shoulders. "I'm sure he's fine, Lucia. You know how Rascon gets sometimes. Needs space to think."

I sent a text. Maybe he wasn't answering anyone else because it was me he needed to hear from. *Where are you? Ma's worried. We're all worried. We need to talk, bro. Just let us know you're okay.* The message showed as delivered but not read.

"He won't miss Christmas," I assured her, even though I wasn't as certain myself.

"I'm sure you're right. He's probably just busy with friends."

I got what she was doing. Find excuses so she didn't go mad with worry.

"Salazar is right," Tryst said with more confidence than I felt. "Rascon will show up tomorrow morning with some explanation that makes perfect sense."

My mother hugged herself. "Let's go inside. It's cold out here."

"Be right in, Ma. I promise."

She kissed my cheek before heading back into the house. The door closed behind her, and the three of us stood in the cold. None of us spoke.

I looked between my brother and uncle. "I don't know what the hell to do."

"About Saffron or Kick?" Bit asked.

"Both."

"You wait." Tryst suggestion surprised me.

"Wait? But tomorrow is—"

He held up a hand. "A day like any other if one is angry and hurt."

"You're right. I can't believe I've managed to destroy two of the most important relationships in my life in the span of a few days."

"You haven't destroyed anything," Bit said. "You've just hit a rough patch."

A rough patch. Like that covered the enormity of what I'd lost tonight. Like a few encouraging words could fix the fact that the woman I loved had kicked me out of her house. The woman I'd planned to propose to.

The ring sat in my truck's glove compartment, where I'd stashed it three weeks ago. I'd imagined a dozen ways to ask her. Down on one knee in the vineyard. Over dinner at the Stonehouse. Somewhere private where it would just be the two of us and I could tell her everything I felt. All I knew for sure was that I had to wait until after the auction. Until the wine sold and the winery was saved and she could breathe again. Until all the weight she'd been carrying lifted and she could actually think about the future instead of just surviving the present.

"I was going to propose," I heard myself say. "Once everything settled down."

Bit's eyes widened, and Tryst's expression softened.

"I wanted everything to be perfect for her." My throat tightened. "To give her the future she deserved. The one where she didn't have to carry everything alone anymore."

"You still can," Bit said.

I shook my head. "She doesn't trust me."

"Then earn it back." He moved closer and put his hand on my shoulder. "Don't give up on the woman you love, Snap. Give her space tonight. Let her process. But then you fight for her. You explain about the bank. You tell her the truth about everything. And you don't stop fighting until she believes you thought what you did was the right thing, but now, you see it might not have been."

"What if she doesn't want to hear it?"

"Then you wait. And you try again. And you keep trying until she does." Bit squeezed my shoulder. "Love isn't about the easy moments. It's about the hard ones. When everything's falling apart and you have to decide if the other person is worth fighting for. Saffron's worth it. You know she is."

He was right. Of course he was right. Saffron was worth every fight, every difficult conversation, every moment of discomfort. She was worth everything.

But knowing that and believing I could fix this weren't the same.

"Come inside," Tryst said. "It's cold, and your mother needs to see you're all right."

"But I'm not."

"She doesn't need to know that tonight. Tomorrow is Christmas. The family is together. Whatever happened with Saffron, whatever's going on with Rascon—those problems will still be there in the morning. Tonight, be present for the people who are here."

I wanted to argue. Wanted to get in my truck and drive to Saffron's house and camp outside her door until she agreed to hear me out. I wanted to track down my brother and make him come home, where he belonged.

But Tryst was right. I couldn't fix any of it tonight.

We walked back to the house together. Inside, warmth and noise enveloped me. Coco ran past, chasing Neva. Both of them were shrieking with laughter. Alex was helping Ma in the kitchen while Maddox and Brix argued about something near the fireplace. Addy sat on the couch with Reagan, reading a book together.

Normal. Everything looked so normal. Like the world hadn't just cracked open and swallowed me whole.

20

Saffron

My hands shook as I slammed my bedroom door hard enough that the frame rattled. I pressed my back against the wood and slid down until I sat on the floor with my knees tight to my chest.

Snapper had lied to me. Kept secrets. And with my sister.

The thought made bile rise in my throat. I'd let him in past every wall I built. I'd fallen in love with him, and he'd been hiding things from me the entire time. My chest felt like someone had reached in and tugged at my heart.

How could he do this? How could Felicity keep their relationship from me? Maybe before he and I were involved, there was no reason for me to know, but my sister knew I was in love with him. How could she say it doesn't matter now? That there was no reason for me to find out?

My phone sat on the nightstand where I'd left it. No messages. Not that I'd expected any. I'd told Snapper to leave, and he had.

A knock sounded at my door.

"Go away."

"We need to talk." Felicity's voice filtered through the wood.

"I said go away."

The door opened anyway. Of course it did. My sister had never been good at respecting my boundaries or— apparently—telling me the truth.

I whirled on her. "You want to talk? Fine. Let's talk about you and Snapper."

Felicity stood on the threshold. Her face went pale, and her eyes widened. "What are you talking about?"

"Don't play dumb with me." I crossed my arms over my chest because it was the only way to keep myself from coming apart at the seams. "Isabel told me about the two of you. She said if I wanted to know what kind of man Snapper really was, I should ask you about your relationship with him."

"Relationship? Saffron, what relationship?"

"The one you had before Wagner. The one you never told me about." My eyes stung, but I blinked the sensation away. "How could you not tell me? You're my sister. We tell each other everything."

Felicity moved into the room and closed the door behind her. She rested against it the same way I had moments ago. "Saffron, listen to me very closely. I was never involved with Snapper. Not ever. Not even close."

"But Isabel said—"

"Isabel lied," Felicity snapped. "That man has been crazy about you since we were teenagers. Everyone knows it. Everyone except you." She pushed away from the door and sat on the edge of my bed. "I would never lie to you. Never. And I sure as hell would never get involved with a man my sister was in love with."

I absorbed what she said, but it felt disconnected from reality. "I'm not—I mean, I wasn't—"

"You've been in love with him for years, Saff. Just like he's been in love with you. Whatever Isabel told you was poison meant to make you doubt him. Don't let her win."

I resumed pacing. "But I heard you. Downstairs. You and Snapper were talking, and you said I didn't need to know. That there was no reason I ever had to know."

Felicity's expression shifted to recognition. "Oh, honey. That wasn't about us. That was about something else."

"What?"

She opened her mouth, then closed it. She looked toward the door like she was making a decision. "I need to tell you something. But I think Mom and Dad should hear it too."

Dread settled in my gut like a stone.

"Just—wait here. I'll be right back."

She disappeared into the hallway before I could argue. I heard her footsteps on the stairs, then muffled voices below. A minute later, footsteps again. Multiple sets this time.

My parents appeared in the doorway with Felicity. My mother's face was lined with concern, and my father looked confused.

"What's going on?" Dad asked.

My sister moved past them into the room. "Isaac Brennan stopped by this afternoon while you were all out."

My dad's eyes opened wide.

"You know I dated him in high school. Anyway, he works at the bank now. In the loan department."

Felicity's gaze moved to our father. "He came to see you, but since you weren't home, he talked to me instead."

"What did he want?" Dad asked.

"To let you know the bank is extending the deadline on the foreclosure."

"Why?" I asked.

"Because they heard about the Christmas Blessing Wine and the upcoming auction. And because, as he said, 'Salazar Avila had committed to cover any shortfall.'"

I gripped the edge of my dresser. "He did what?"

"Snapper went to the bank. He made a deal with Isaac. If the wine didn't work out and for whatever reason there wasn't enough money to cover the debt—Snapper guaranteed he'd cover the difference."

Air refused to fill my lungs properly. My thoughts scattered in a dozen directions.

"He was going to pay off our family's debt?" The question came out as a whisper. "Without telling me?"

"Without telling any of us," my dad added. "Not unlike you, Saffron."

His words stung, but I knew he was right. I was angry with Snapper for doing the same thing I had.

"That's what we were talking about downstairs." When Felicity patted the bed beside her and held out her hand, I sat down. "I told him about Isaac's visit and thanked him for offering to help our family. He said he thought he should tell you, and I convinced him there was no reason to. If there's anyone you should be angry with, it's me, not him."

"I was so awful to him…"

"Go to him." My mother sat on my other side. "Apologize."

"What if he won't listen?"

Felicity gripped my hand. "He'll listen. Believe me."

But I couldn't go. Not yet. Not when my mind was still spinning and my heart was still racing and everything I thought I knew had just been turned inside out.

"I need time to think," I said.

My parents and Felicity exchanged glances, but they didn't argue. They left one by one until I was alone again in my room with the weight of what I'd learned pressing down on my chest.

I lay down and stared at the ceiling. The house had gone quiet. Everyone else had retreated to their rooms or to bed. Outside my window, the night was dark and still, and my mind wouldn't stop racing.

Isabel had lied. She'd planted doubt in my head, and I'd let it grow. I'd let it poison my thoughts until I couldn't see the truth that was right in front of me. Snapper had never been involved with Felicity. The idea was absurd. Felicity would've told me. And even if she hadn't, I would've known. I would've seen them together.

And God, Snapper had been showing me how he felt for months. Years, maybe.

I should have had the guts to ask them both directly.

While the arrangement he made with the bank was different, he'd still gone behind my back. My first instinct was to be angry about it. To feel like he'd overstepped or tried to control things he had no right to. He'd made a financial commitment without telling me or my family. Both he and the people at the bank were wrong for doing that. On some level, it was probably illegal, not that that kind of thing always mattered in a small, tight-knit town. If it had gotten as far as foreclosure, then my parents would've had to be notified, obviously.

But what he'd done had been out of love. Because he couldn't stand the thought of us losing everything.

Because he wanted to give me a safety net even if I never knew it existed.

It was stupid and overprotective and exactly the kind of thing someone did when they loved another person so much they couldn't help themselves.

I rolled onto my side and got in the fetal position. The memory of Thanksgiving came flooding back. We'd been at Felicity's house. In the guest room. In bed together after making love.

"Saffron, I love—" he'd started.

And I'd kissed him. Cut him off before he could finish. Because I hadn't been ready to hear it, say it back, or admit that what we had was real and permanent.

But even then, he'd been showing me in actions since October. Finding the formula with me. Convincing his family to help. Harvesting the grapes side by side. Making the wine. Holding me when fear and doubt crept in. All of it had been out of love.

And what had I done? I'd kicked him out. Told him to leave. Refused to let him tell his side of the story.

Fresh tears spilled down my cheeks and soaked into my pillow. I'd been so scared of needing him. So terrified of depending on someone else. So convinced that letting him in would make me weak.

But needing someone didn't make me weak. It made me human.

I reached for my phone on the nightstand. It was after midnight. I couldn't call him now. What I needed to say should be done in person anyway. I closed my eyes, but sleep wouldn't come. Three in the morning came and went. Then four.

Around five, I gave up trying to sleep. I sat up in bed and grabbed my phone again. Still nothing from Snapper. Not that I'd expected there to be. I threw back the covers and stood. My legs felt shaky, but I went to my closet and put on jeans and a sweater, then to the bathroom where I ran a comb through my hair, washed my face, and brushed my teeth.

In the mirror, I looked like hell. My eyes were red and swollen. My face was pale. But it didn't matter.

I grabbed my keys and my phone and crept downstairs, thankful that the house was quiet and everyone was still asleep.

Outside, the air was cold enough to make me shiver. The horizon showed the first hints of dawn, but darkness still claimed most of the sky. I climbed into my truck and started the engine.

I knew Snapper would be at his mother's house rather than his own since he'd told me it was tradition for the whole family to stay on the estate and wake up together on Christmas morning. I also knew that if she wasn't awake already, Lucia would soon be in the kitchen, making breakfast. If she didn't know already, I'd tell her that Snapper and I had had a falling out and ask to speak with him. No doubt she'd take me up to his room herself.

The gates of Los Caballeros appeared ahead, and I turned in and followed the familiar road to the main house. Lights glowed in the downstairs windows. Someone was awake, most likely Lucia, as I'd anticipated.

I parked, cut the engine, then sat there for several seconds, trying to steady my breathing.

I saw movement on the porch from the corner of my eye—Snapper coming out the door. My heart stopped, then started again, faster than before.

It was five-thirty in the morning on Christmas yet he was standing outside, watching me.

I climbed out of my truck and walked toward him. Each step felt monumental. The cold air bit at my exposed skin, and my breath clouded in front of my face. The horizon was starting to lighten now. Dawn was coming.

"Saffron?"

"I couldn't sleep." I stopped near the bottom of the porch steps and looked up at him. "You?"

"Me either."

We stared at each other. Neither of us moved.

"Can I come up?" I asked.

"Of course."

I climbed the steps, but maintained distance between us even though everything in me wanted to throw myself into his arms and bury my face against his chest and tell him I was sorry for everything.

"I need to explain why I reacted the way I did."

"Okay."

"As you know, Isabel came to see me a few weeks ago." I wrapped my arms around myself. "She suggested I ask Felicity about your relationship with her."

Snapper's eyes scrunched. "Saffron, Felicity and I—"

"I know. Isabel lied." As hard as it was, I forced myself to continue. "When I heard the two of you talking, that's what I thought it was about."

"I was never involved with Felicity. Not ever. Not even close. There's never been anyone but you, Saff. Not in any way that mattered."

"I know. Felicity told me what you were really talking about." Tears spilled down my cheeks. "But regardless, I should have asked instead of assuming. I should have let you explain instead of telling you to leave."

He took a step toward me. Then stopped.

"I know about your arrangement with the bank." I watched his expression shift. Guilt flickered across his face before he steeled it and looked away.

"I was going to tell you. After the auction. After everything was resolved."

"Why didn't you tell me before?"

"Because you would have refused my help. And even if you didn't, your father would have. And then, you would have felt obligated to me. Like you owed me something." His jaw clenched. "I wanted you to choose me because you wanted to, not because you felt like you had to."

My heart broke and mended at the same time. "Snapper—"

"I know I handled it wrong, but I couldn't just sit by and watch your family's legacy disappear."

I stepped closer and reached up and cupped his face with both hands. "You were trying to protect me. Protect my family."

His eyes met mine. "I…I care about you, Saffron."

"I know. I care about you too. I was just too scared to admit it. Too scared to need you as much as I do."

"And now?"

"I'm done being scared." I rose up on my toes and pressed my lips to his. "I'm so sorry. For not trusting you. For telling you to leave. For not letting you explain."

"I'm sorry I didn't tell you."

I looked him in the eyes. "You're forgiven. For everything."

He put his arms around me and gathered me close enough that our bodies were flush. "Do you mean that?"

"Absolutely."

"At Thanksgiving," he began, "I tried to tell you something."

"I remember." I said barely above a whisper. "I stopped you. I wasn't ready to hear it."

"Are you ready now?"

"I am."

His thumbs traced along my cheekbones. "I love you, Saffron Hope. I've loved you for so long I don't remember what it felt like not to love you."

The words washed over me and through me, filling the hollow places inside me that I hadn't known were empty.

"I love you too. I have for so long. I was just too stubborn to admit it."

His mouth moved warm against mine with a kiss that was gentle, deep, emotional, and healing. When we broke apart, both of us had tears in our eyes.

"I was going to wait," Snapper said. "Until after the auction. Until everything was resolved and you could breathe again."

"Wait for what?"

He reached into his pocket and took out a small box.

"Snapper?"

He opened it.

The ring inside stole what little breath I had left. Even in the weak dawn light, it caught every ray and threw it back transformed. The center stone was larger than anything I would have chosen for myself—but it didn't look ostentatious. It looked right. The band was what made fresh tears flood my eyes. Delicate vines wrapped around the stone and intertwined with each other. Grapevines. Our heritage. Our livelihood. Our story etched in precious metal.

My hands flew to my mouth, and my trembling fingers pressed against my lips as if I could hold in the sob that wanted to escape.

Snapper got down on one knee on his mother's porch. "Saffron Hope." His voice was steady even though his hands weren't. "I've loved you since before I knew what love meant. You're my best friend. My partner. The woman I want to spend forever with." He took a deep breath and let it out slowly. "You challenge me," he continued. "You inspire me. You make me want to be better. You call me out on my shit, and you steal food off my plate, and you sing off-key without caring who hears."

A laugh escaped me.

"You're stubborn and independent, and you'd rather break than bend. You carry the weight of the world on your shoulders and refuse to let anyone help. You work yourself to exhaustion and then get up the next morning and do it all over again because that's who you are."

More tears. My vision blurred, but I could still see him. Still see the ring. Still see this moment crystallizing into memory.

"I can't imagine my life without you in it. I don't want to imagine it. I want to wake up next to you every morning. I want to make wine with you. I want to watch you become an aunt to a dozen more nieces and nephews and a mother to our children. I want to fight with you and make up with you and grow old with you."

He paused and swallowed hard.

"I want to be the person you turn to when everything falls apart. The one you reach for when you're scared. The one you celebrate with when things go right. I want to be your partner in every way. For the rest of my life. Will you marry me?"

"Yes." My answer burst out of me. "Yes. Yes, absolutely yes."

His smile transformed his whole face. Relief and joy and love all mixed together in an expression so beautiful it made my chest ache.

I held out my left hand when he removed the ring from the box. Snapper steadied my hand with his and slid the band onto my finger.

"It's so beautiful," I whispered, then fell to my knees and kissed him. It felt deeper this time. We were engaged. We were getting married. We were promising each other forever on Christmas morning while the sun rose and the world woke up around us.

His hands tangled in my hair. Mine gripped his shoulders. We kissed like we could communicate everything we felt through touch alone. Like words weren't enough to hold the enormity of what we'd just promised each other.

When we broke apart, we were both breathing hard.

"Merry Christmas," I whispered against his mouth.

"Best Christmas ever." He wrapped his arms around me. "Though I have to say, this isn't how I imagined proposing."

"No?"

"I had a whole plan. Dinner at the Stonehouse. Candles. Music. Romance." He pressed a kiss to the top of my head. "This was much better."

I laughed. "Your mom is going to lose her mind."

"She's going to cry tears of happiness all day long."

"Your brothers are going to give you so much shit."

"Worth it." He leaned away enough to look at me. "You're worth everything, Saff."

Fresh tears spilled down my cheeks. "I love you so much."

"I love you too, sweetheart."

"We should probably go inside," he said, standing then holding out his hand to help me up. "Before my family sees us out here and starts asking questions."

"Too late for that."

He followed my gaze to the window. Lucia was there, watching us with her hands pressed to her mouth. Even from this distance, I could see tears on her cheeks.

When we walked inside, Lucia rushed to meet us. *"Mijo! Mija!"* She pulled us both into a hug that squeezed the air from my lungs. "You're engaged! Oh my God, you're engaged!"

"Ma, we just—"

"I know! I have eyes, Salazar." She grabbed my left hand and studied the ring. "It's beautiful. It's perfect. You're perfect together." She hugged me again. "Welcome to the family, *mija*. Welcome home."

"What's going on?" Brix asked, coming around the corner. His eyes landed on my hand, and his face broke into a huge grin. "No way."

"Yes way." Snapper held me tight against his side. "Saffron said yes."

Soon, the kitchen was crowded with the rest of his family. There were shouts of congratulations, hugs, and tears. Even Snapper's nieces and nephews crowded around us, and Coco tugged on my sleeve. "Does this mean you're getting married?"

"It does."

She bounced on her toes. "Can I be a flower girl?"

I hugged her hard. "Of course you can."

Neva stared at the ring with wide eyes. "Pretty."

"Very pretty," I agreed.

Bit stepped forward, and when his eyes landed on my ring, his face split into a huge smile. "It's about damn time."

"Shut up," Snapper said, but he was grinning too.

"Eberly owes me fifty bucks. I said you'd propose by Christmas. She said New Year's."

Snapper's brow furrowed. "You were betting on us?"

"Everyone was betting on you two." Bit embraced me. "Welcome to the family, Saffron. Fair warning— we're loud and obnoxious, and we're in each other's business all the time."

"I wouldn't have it any other way."

The sound of a vehicle approaching made everyone go still. Lucia raced to the window and gasped. "Thank the Lord, it's Rascon."

"Give me a minute?" Snapper asked.

"Of course."

Lucia motioned for me to stand next to her, and we watched as the two brothers held onto each other for several seconds. Then, the two came inside. Kick looked terrible. Like he hadn't slept in days. His clothes were rumpled, his hair was a mess, and his eyes were red—but he was smiling. His eyes dropped to my left hand. "Holy shit. You're engaged."

"As of about twenty minutes ago."

"Congratulations," he said, hugging me. "Take care of my brother. He's an idiot, but he's my idiot."

"Hey," Snapper protested.

"It's true, and you know it."

The tension broke, and everyone laughed first, then took turns embracing him.

Snapper stepped closer and whispered in my ear. "You okay?"

"I'm perfect." I turned and kissed him. "Absolutely perfect."

And for the first time in months, I meant it.

Snapper

Sterling Creek Winery's event space looked much the same as it had the night of the Wicked Winemakers' Ball, except rather than a dinner followed by a bachelor auction—one I hoped to never be in again—tonight, a wine auction was taking place. Display cases lined the walls, each holding bottles of Christmas Blessing Wine that gleamed under spotlights. Two thousand bottles, numbered and authenticated, ready to be sold to the highest bidders.

The room was full of people I knew and more I didn't. Baron Van Orr's PR team had managed what seemed impossible in the short time he had to publicize tonight's event.

On the other hand, that we had extraordinary wine to sell had been a far more difficult feat.

I found Saffron standing near the entrance, arms crossed, jaw tight.

"Stop catastrophizing," I said.

Her gaze met mine. "I'm not."

"You're chewing your bottom lip."

"That's not catastrophizing; that's anxiety."

"Same thing." I moved her hand away from where she'd been twisting her engagement ring. "It's going to work."

"You keep saying that."

"I keep meaning it."

Lucas emerged from the back room where he'd been coordinating with the auction house staff. Baron Van Orr was with him, both men looking more relaxed and having more fun than I'd ever seen them.

"Sixty minutes to showtime," Lucas said. "And we're ready."

Baron held up a glossy catalog that told the story of three families reuniting after seventy years. "The PR firm says there are far more international investors than they anticipated."

"That's good, right?" Saffron asked.

"That's excellent." Baron set the catalog on a nearby table. "The pre-auction buzz has been stronger than anything I've seen in twenty years of attending these events."

"What if it's all hype?" Saffron asked. "What if people show up, taste it, and decide it's not worth the excitement?"

"Then, they're idiots." Lucas put his hand on his daughter's shoulder. "But, Saffron, stop second-guessing yourself." He motioned to where tasting tables had been set up. "Do the reactions over there look like the wine is anything less than extraordinary?"

When she returned to chewing her bottom lip, her father put his arm around her shoulders. "Believe in yourself, daughter."

"Easier said than done," I heard her mutter.

The next hour crawled. The auction house staff reviewed bidding procedures and payment processing while a wine journalist from a major publication arrived to photograph the bottles and interview Baron about his grandmother's role in the original blend.

I stayed close to Saffron, one hand on the small of her back, grounding both of us while chaos swirled around us.

The energy in the room shifted as guests took their seats. This was real. This was happening.

I looked over and saw Ma sweep in with Tryst, Jaicon, my siblings, and their spouses. The only person noticeably missing tonight was Isabel Van Orr, not that we knew why she chose not to attend.

"Tonight is your night, *mija*," my mother said, pulling Saffron into a hug. "Enjoy every second."

"I'm trying not to throw up," she admitted.

"That's normal. I threw up before my wedding." Ma patted her cheek. "You'll be fine."

I gathered my fiancée in my arms and kissed her.

"Stop being weird," Kick said, bumping into me.

"Kissing my future bride is not weird."

"Whatever," he muttered before walking away.

Felicity and Wagner arrived with Diana. The sisters hugged and cried a little, then laughed at themselves for crying. Wagner kept checking his phone for updates from the babysitter watching Beatrice, and Felicity kept telling him to relax.

"She's fine," Saffron said. "Stop worrying."

"Says the woman who's been pacing for two hours," Felicity shot back.

The stragglers at the tasting tables took their seats when the auctioneer announced he'd get started in five minutes.

"The balance is remarkable for such a young wine," one collector said to his companion as they walked by.

"That aged component bridges everything," someone else said.

"Exemplary vintage," said another woman. "I've been collecting wine for forty years, and I've never encountered anything quite like this."

Saffron heard that last comment, and her grip on my hand tightened. "They really love it."

"Of course they do. It's a masterpiece."

"Our masterpiece," she said.

"Ours," I agreed.

At seven o'clock sharp, the auctioneer took the stage. The man was a friend of Baron's who had decades of experience working high-end wine auctions.

"Welcome. Tonight, we're offering two thousand bottles of the Christmas Blessing Wine, recreated after seventy years. A significant portion of tonight's proceeds has been designated for local charities." After those in the room applauded, he held up his gavel. "Let's begin."

The first lot was a single bottle. Bidding opened at five hundred dollars.

A paddle went up immediately. Then another. Within thirty seconds, the price had doubled.

"One thousand," the auctioneer called. "Do I hear twelve hundred?"

More paddles.

"Fifteen hundred. Do I hear two thousand?"

The bidding climbed faster than I'd anticipated. Two thousand became twenty-five hundred, then three thousand. Collectors competed with the kind of intensity usually reserved for rare Bordeaux or aged Burgundy.

The gavel came down at thirty-two hundred dollars for a single bottle.

Saffron swayed beside me, and I tightened my arm around her waist.

"That's just the start," I whispered.

Case lots went next. Six and twelve bottles had been packaged together for collectors who wanted volume. The bidding was even more competitive. The first case of twelve opened at fifteen thousand and sold for twenty-eight thousand. The second went for thirty-one thousand. The third hit thirty-eight thousand, and the room erupted in more applause.

"This is insane," Saffron said under her breath.

"This is success."

I glanced around the room while the bidding continued. My family stood together on the left side, every one of them watching with expressions that ranged from pride to disbelief. Lucas and Diana were with Baron on the right, and my future father-in-law had tears spilling over on his cheeks that he wiped away as quickly as he could.

The auction continued for two hours. Single bottles, cases, larger lots for restaurants and wine programs. Every lot exceeded its estimated value. Some by double. The energy in the room increased with each pound of the gavel.

"This is the final lot of the evening," the auctioneer announced. "Twelve bottles with sequential numbers from the heart of the production run. These are some of the finest bottles in the entire collection. Opening bid is twenty thousand dollars."

Paddles shot up around the room. More than I could count.

"Twenty-five thousand. Do I hear thirty?"

Another paddle.

"Thirty-five thousand. Do I hear forty?"

The bidding climbed in five-thousand-dollar increments. Forty became forty-five, then fifty. At fifty-five thousand, half the paddles dropped out. At sixty thousand, only three bidders remained.

"Sixty-five thousand," the auctioneer called. "Do I hear sixty-eight?"

A paddle went up in the back corner.

"Sixty-eight thousand. Going once." He raised his gavel. "Going twice." Pause. "Sold for sixty-eight thousand dollars."

The gavel came down, and the room exploded in applause.

The auctioneer asked for a moment to tally the final totals. The buzz of conversation filled the space while we waited. Speculation ran rampant—three million, maybe three and a half, possibly four.

Saffron's hand shook in mine. I brought it to my lips and kissed her knuckles.

"Whatever the number is, we won," I said quietly.

"I know. I just—I'm having a hard time taking it all in. Believing it's real."

"It is, Saff, and so are we."

The auctioneer returned to the stage, and the room went silent.

"Ladies and gentlemen, I'm pleased to announce that the final total for this evening's auction of the Christmas Blessing Wine is four point two million dollars."

Applause thundered off the stone walls. People were on their feet, cheering, and celebrating not just the wine but the story behind it.

Saffron gasped and covered her mouth with both hands. Her eyes filled, and tears streaked down her cheeks.

Lucas pushed through the crowd and lifted Saffron off her feet. Both of them were crying, holding each other like they were afraid to let go. Diana joined them seconds later, wrapping her arms around them as the celebration continued.

Ma found me and hugged me hard enough to crack ribs. "I'm so proud of you, *mijo*. So incredibly proud."

"Thanks, Ma."

"Your father would be proud too. Of the man you've become. Of what you did for this family."

My throat closed, and I couldn't speak, so I just hugged her tighter.

Tryst appeared next and gripped my shoulder. "Well done, nephew."

"Couldn't have done it without Los Caballeros," I said quietly enough that only he could hear.

"That's what the brotherhood is for."

While our family and Baron offered to let the Hopes keep all the proceeds, Lucas wouldn't hear of it. He insisted the profits be split three ways, and we agreed. Given the total raised, I had no doubt a one-third share wouldn't just cover their debt; it would give them operating capital well into the future.

While payments were processed, we moved to a private room Sterling Creek had set aside for post-auction celebration. Champagne appeared, and glasses were distributed to everyone.

Tryst raised his glass first. "To family. To friendship. To partnerships that transcend generations and heal old wounds."

"To family," we echoed, and the sound of glasses clinking filled the room.

Lucas stood next. He looked around at the faces of the three families that were reunited after seventy years apart.

"When I thought everything was lost, when I'd accepted we would lose the winery, Saffron refused to give up. She found her great-grandmother's journal, and she saw a possibility." He turned to look at Saffron directly. "But she didn't do it alone. She partnered with the Avila family, who gave their grapes and their expertise and their faith. She worked with Baron Van Orr, whose family's contribution completed what our grandmothers started. This wine exists because three families chose to come together instead of staying apart."

He raised his glass higher. "To partnerships. To faith. To second chances."

"To second chances," many of us murmured in response.

Baron stepped forward. "My grandmother made a choice seventy years ago that she regretted for the rest of her life. Tonight, that wrong has been righted. The Christmas Blessing Wine lives again, and with it, Ellen Van Orr's legacy is transformed from regret to redemption. Thank you for allowing my family to be a part of this."

He raised his glass and drank, and the room followed.

Brix spoke next about brotherhood and supporting your own. Alex talked about taking risks and believing in impossible things.

Saffron and I slipped out onto a small balcony that overlooked Sterling's vineyard, and I wrapped my arms around her from behind as we looked out on the moonlit vines.

"You did it," I said into her hair.

She laughed and cried at the same time. "No, we did." She turned in my arms to face me. "I couldn't have done any of this without you. Without your family. Without everyone who believed in something that seemed impossible two months ago."

"Nothing's impossible when you're stubborn enough."

That got a real laugh. "Are you calling me stubborn?"

"Absolutely. It's one of my favorite things about you."

She leaned up and kissed me. The kind of kiss that made the rest of the world disappear, that reminded me exactly why I'd fallen in love with this woman in the first place.

"I love you," she whispered against my mouth.

"I love you too, Saff."

We stayed out there for several more minutes, holding each other while the party continued inside. The winter air was cold, but I barely felt it. All I felt was Saffron, warm against me, her heart beating in rhythm with mine, our future spreading out before us.

Eventually, we went back inside and rejoined the celebration. Hours passed in laughter and champagne and relief so complete it left me dizzy.

By the time midnight rolled around, most of the guests had left. Only family remained—my siblings and their spouses, Saffron's parents and sister, Baron, Tryst, and Jaicon. We stood in small groups, talking quietly, exhausted but too elated to leave.

Kick found Saffron and me near one of the now-empty display cases. "Hey. I just wanted to say congratulations again. Tonight was incredible."

"Thanks." I studied my brother. "You okay?"

"Yeah, I'm good. Just—" He paused. "I'm really happy for you both. The way you brought all that together, the wine, the auction, everything."

"We couldn't have done it without you," Saffron said. "Without everyone."

Baron appeared then, crossing the room toward us. His face was troubled in a way I hadn't seen all evening.

"Sorry to interrupt, but, Kick, have you heard from Isabel?" he asked.

My brother's brow furrowed. "No, not since I took her to the airport a few days ago. Why?"

"Did she say where she was going?"

"Your villa in Italy." Kick's head cocked. "She said she'd be there through mid-January. Is something wrong?"

Baron's face went pale. "She never arrived."

Keep reading for a sneak peek

at the next book in the

Wicked Winemakers Central Coast

Second Label series,

Kick's Kiss

Their secret romance ended badly—with bitter words neither can take back. She's disappeared to start over where scandal can't touch her. He's found her anyway, and this time, he's not walking away—no matter what she's hiding.

KICK

When Isabel Van Orr disappears after our family's wine auction instead of flying to Italy, I volunteer to track her down. What I don't tell anyone is that Isabel and I had a secret relationship that ended badly, and I'm the reason she's running. When I find her working at a winery in the Russian River Valley, she begs me to leave. But the fear in her eyes tells me she's hiding something bigger than embarrassment. So I make her a deal: let me stay and prove I'm not the man she thinks I am, and after she tells me the truth, I'll walk away if that's what she wants. The problem? The longer I stay, the more I realize leaving her is the last thing I'll ever do.

ISABEL

I've spent years being "that pathetic woman" who publicly chased Snapper Avila, so when I fell into a secret relationship with his younger brother, Kick, I thought I'd finally found someone who saw the real me. Then I nearly sabotaged his family's wine project out of jealousy, proved him right about my worst qualities, and we ended things badly. Weeks later, everything changed. Rather than face the humiliation and judgment waiting for me at home, I disappeared to a small town where no one knows my name. But Kick tracks me down, sees through my lies, and refuses to leave. Now, I'm faced with an impossible choice: keep running and protect myself from the scandal that will destroy what's left of my reputation, or trust the man I love with the secret that could bind us together forever—or tear us apart when his family learns the truth.

Prologue

Kick

I found Isabel Van Orr on a Sunday morning, nine days after I'd dropped her off at the airport. Four days after her father told me she'd never arrived in Italy.

She was pruning vines in the back section of the Whitmore Estate Vineyards, five hours north of Paso Robles, wearing work clothes I'd never seen her in and an expression of fierce concentration that disappeared the second she looked up and saw me.

For a moment, we stared at each other across ten feet of vineyard rows. Her face went white, then red, then she dropped the pruning shears and ran.

"Isabel!" I broke into a sprint. "Stop!"

She cut through the vines toward an equipment barn on the far side of the property, moving fast despite the uneven ground.

I was faster.

I caught her arm and spun her around. She crashed into my chest, and for one terrible, wonderful second, every reason I had for ending things between us evaporated. All I felt was relief that she was alive, that I'd found her.

Then she shoved against my chest. "Let go of me."

"Not until you tell me what's going on." I didn't release her. Couldn't. "You're supposed to be in Italy. I drove you to the airport myself."

"I lied." She wrenched free and put distance between us. "How did you find me? Does anyone else know I'm here?"

Panic flickered across her face. "You can't tell my father where I am."

"Isabel! He deserves to know you're alive."

"Then tell him that but not where I am."

I took a step closer. She took one back.

"What are you running from, Isabel?"

"I'm not running—"

"You're terrified. I can see it. Tell me why."

She laughed, but the sound came out broken. "You don't know me as well as you think you do."

"Wrong. You're not as good an actress as you think you are."

"Why are you here?" The question burst out of her. "You made it very clear what you thought of me. I'm spoiled and—"

"When I said those things, I was angry and scared you'd hurt people I care about. And I apologized. More than once."

"It doesn't matter now." She turned away. "You need to go."

"What are you doing working at Whitmore? If he finds out who—"

"He knows exactly who I am and he hired me anyway." Her eyes filled with tears she blinked away. "Please, Kick. If you ever cared about me at all, just go. Tell my father I'm alive. Tell him I'll come home when I'm ready. But don't tell him where I am."

"When will you be ready?"

"I don't know."

The gaze she leveled at me was the closest she came to looking like the Isabel I'd known most of my life.

I should walk away. Respect her wishes and leave her to whatever she was trying to do. But every instinct I had was screaming that something was very wrong. That whatever had sent her here had nothing to do with her dad.

"Just go. Please."

"No," I said.

She blinked. "What?"

"I'm not leaving. You want to stay here and hide? Fine. But I'm staying too."

"That's insane."

"Probably." I crossed my arms. "But I'm not going back to Paso Robles without getting some answers. And I'm sure as hell not leaving you alone when you look like you haven't slept since I last saw you." I pulled out my phone.

"What are you doing?"

"Calling Baron. Not to tell him where you are—but to tell him you're safe and you're with me."

"Kick—"

I was already dialing. Baron answered on the first ring.

"Did you find her?"

"Yes. She's safe and she's with me."

"Where?" His voice was sharp. "I'll send someone—"

"She doesn't want to come home yet. She needs time."

A long silence. "Time." The word came out flat, controlled. "Is this about the trust fund? Tell her if she thinks running away will change my mind—"

"This isn't about money."

"Everything with Isabel is about money. Or attention." Another pause. "What's she doing? Who's she with?"

"She's working—"

"Working?" His laugh was bitter. "My daughter has never worked a day in her life."

"She's safe, Baron. That's what matters."

"What matters is she disappeared without a word. Do you know how that looks? Jesus, now I have to call the sheriff and tell him she's okay." His voice hardened. "You tell her she has two weeks to stop this nonsense and come home. After that, I'm cutting her off completely."

About the Author

USA Today best-selling author Heather Slade writes shamelessly sexy, edge-of-your seat romantic suspense.

She gave herself the gift of writing a book for her own birthday one year. Sixty-plus books later (and counting), she's having the time of her life.

The women Slade writes are self-confident, strong, with wills of their own, and hearts as big as the Colorado sky. The men are sublimely sexy, seductive alphas who rise to the challenge of capturing the sweet soul of a woman whose heart they'll hold in the palm of their hand forever. Add in a couple of neck-snapping twists and turns, a page-turning mystery, and a swoon-worthy HEA, and you'll be holding one of her books in your hands.

She loves to hear from her readers. You can contact her at heather@heatherslade.com

To keep up with her latest news and releases, please visit her website at www.heatherslade.com to sign up for her newsletter.

MORE FROM AUTHOR HEATHER SLADE

WINE COUNTRY ROMANCE

BUTLER RANCH
Kade's Worth
Brodie's Promise
Maddox's Truce
Naughton's Secret
Mercer's Vow
Kade's Return
Butler Ranch Christmas

WICKED WINEMAKERS
CENTRAL COAST
FIRST LABEL
Brix's Bid
Ridge's Release
Press' Passion
Zin's Sins
Tryst's Temptation

WICKED WINEMAKERS
CENTRAL COAST
SECOND LABEL
Beau's Beloved
Cru's Crush
Bit's Bliss
Snapper's Seduction
Kick's Kiss

WICKED WINEMAKERS
RUSSIAN RIVER VALLEY
FIRST LABEL
Bas' Blend
Hux's Harvest
Wolf's Want
Oak's Vintage
Cooper's Claim

COWBOY ROMANCE

COWBOYS OF
CRESTED BUTTE
A Cowboy Falls
A Cowboy's Dance
A Cowboy's Kiss
A Cowboy Stays
A Cowboy Wins

ROARING FORK RANCH
Roaring Fork Wrangler
Roaring Fork Roughstock
Roaring Fork Rockstar
Roaring Fork Rooker
Roaring Fork Bridger

SANGRE VISTA RANCH
Thorn's Stand
Stetson's Storm
Maverick's Reckoning
Cinch's Wager
Flints Chance

9 79888 6 491128